"You do not seem terrified," Ana said.

"I'm a man," Ryder said, his mouth quirking up at one corner in an expression she found oddly endearing. "Not a mouse."

He certainly was that. A different sort of man than she was used to in her life. He was strong, competent and clearly brave. Trustworthy? She thought so. He was doing the right thing, that was clear. But there was so much she didn't know. There were hidden depths to him that she did not understand, and she had no time to plumb them now.

That she wanted to unsettled her.

Dear Reader,

I love interconnected stories, and continuity series are always challenging and fun. Keeping the details straight between a bunch of authors who all have their own approach is daunting, and my hat's off to any editor who can manage it.

When Silhouette Books asked me to participate in this revisit to THE COLTONS, I was given a description that began with the phrase, "Bad-boy hero…" Well, anyone who's read my work knows that's a theme I thrive on, and it didn't take much more than that to get me on board. Ryder Colton is indeed a bad boy, but one who's been given another chance to get it right, giving me the chance to revisit another favorite theme. Throw in a strong, determined, smart woman, and let the magic of redemption begin!

Ryder and Ana's story was an emotional one to write, and I hope it reaches you, too.

Enjoy this episode of THE COLTONS: FAMILY FIRST!

Happy reading!

Justine Davis

JUSTINE DAVIS

Baby's Watch

Special thanks and acknowledgment to
Justine Davis for her contribution to
The Coltons: Family First miniseries.

ISBN-13: 978-0-373-27614-1
ISBN-10: 0-373-27614-1

BABY'S WATCH

This edition published by arrangement with Harlequin Books S.A.

Visit Silhouette Books at www.eHarlequin.com

Printed in U.S.A.

Books by Justine Davis

Silhouette Romantic Suspense

Wicked Secrets #555
Left at the Altar #596
Out of the Dark #638
The Morning Side of Dawn #674
†*Lover Under Cover* #698
†*Leader of the Pack* #728
†*A Man To Trust* #805
†*Gage Butler's Reckoning* #841
†*Badge of Honor* #871
†*Clay Yeager's Redemption* #926
The Return of Luke McGuire #1036
**Just Another Day in Paradise* #1141
The Prince's Wedding #1190
**One of These Nights* #1201
**In His Sights* #1318
**Second-Chance Hero* #1351
**Dark Reunion* #1452
**Deadly Temptation* #1493
**Her Best Friend's Husband* #1525
Backstreet Hero #1539
Baby's Watch #1544

†Trinity Street West
*Redstone, Incorporated

JUSTINE DAVIS

lives on Puget Sound in Washington. Her interests outside of writing are sailing, doing needlework, horseback riding and driving her restored 1967 Corvette roadster—top down, of course.

Justine says that years ago, during her career in law enforcement, a young man she worked with encouraged her to try for a promotion to a position that was at the time occupied only by men. "I succeeded, became wrapped up in my new job, and that man moved away—never, I thought, to be heard from again. Ten years later he appeared out of the woods of Washington state, saying he'd never forgotten me and would I please marry him. With that history, how could I write anything but romance?"

Chapter 1

Cops, federal agents and the people who wrote glamorous stories about them, were all crazy. There was freaking nothing glamorous about undercover work, Ryder Colton mused as he stubbed out his last cigar.

In fact, he thought wryly, the only difference between his life right now and his life seven months ago was that now he was sitting in the dark in a stand of scrub brush, unable to leave, instead of in a cell at the Lone Star Correctional Facility, unable to leave.

Well, that and the cigar, he amended silently. He'd missed the taste of the Texas-born Little Travis cigars he'd gotten attached to when he'd started running with the older and greatly admired Bart Claymore at fifteen, and bummed them from him.

Bart was one of the men who'd left him holding the bag the night that had started him on the road to prison—an irony that wasn't lost on him. Then there was the irony of his entire situation: that he, the bad boy of the Texas Coltons, was here pretending to be one of the good guys. Near the end—or so he hoped—of his search. A search that had brought him back to, of all places, the Bar None ranch. Now that was irony.

And *irony* was a word he'd never used in his life before now. He only vaguely remembered a discussion of it in some class in school, before he'd landed himself in juvie detention the first time. He must have paid more attention than he'd thought, because now, all of a sudden, it made perfect sense.

You're smarter than you want to believe.

Boots's words echoed in Ryder's head. The first time he'd said them, Ryder had laughed in his face; he never would have pegged the leathery, prison-toughened convict as a do-gooder. But Boots Johnson hadn't been the first one to tell Ryder he was smarter than he was acting. He'd heard the litany countless times before, from teachers, counselors, and family—especially Clay.

Ryder winced inwardly at the memory of his straight-arrow, stiff-spined brother. Clay had done his best when their mother had died, leaving the eighteen-year-old with a fourteen-year-old sister and a sixteen-year-old brother he had tried to take care of. Georgie had turned out okay, her only mistake was falling for that city slicker. But that had given her little Emmie, the pride and joy of her life.

His niece.

He remembered the moment when he'd told Boots about her.

So, you're an uncle, the old man had said.

He'd blinked, opened his mouth to say "What?" then shut it again. Emmie had been born well over a year before he'd landed here, and until that moment he'd never thought of himself as an uncle. A relative. Connected.

Not that his sister would want her now five-year-old little girl connected to him. Georgie was too determined that her little girl have a good life, and somehow he doubted that plan would include an uncle convicted of a felony who'd been in the federal pen most of her young life.

He considered lighting another cigar and decided against it; he only had a few more, and they were hard to come by. If nothing else, he'd learned in prison that his live-as-if-there-were-no-tomorrow philosophy wasn't always the best policy. And his motto—have your fun today—had landed him in a very tight spot.

Thankfully, the sky was getting lighter now, so he had to pack it in. He was tired from lack of sleep, also from the endless hours of sitting, watching, waiting for something that didn't happen.

And thinking. Most of all, he was tired of the thinking, the contemplating, the pondering. His brother had been the thinker of the family—not him. But sitting out here all night long, there was nothing else to do.

And he knew now why he'd always avoided it. It was much easier to just live his life, doing what seemed like a good idea at the time…

"And look where that landed you," he told himself as he buried the stub of his last cigar and headed back to the ten-year-old, battered pickup he was driving these days. They'd offered him a standard-issue, plain-wrap sedan, which he had wryly told them would stand out in Texas ranch country like a neon sign.

"Why don't you just paint Narc on the side and be done with it?" he'd said, earning him a frown from Furnell, his main handler.

Handler. That's actually what they called him. That had been the sourest bite in this whole stupid meal. Ryder Colton, the man who never let anybody, man or woman, "handle" him, not even his own family, was now owned by a dark-suited, overly tense type A. At least, he was for now.

And if that wasn't bad enough, he wasn't even watching for drug runners or murderers, nothing dramatic or exciting like that.

No, Ryder Colton, the bad boy of the Texas Coltons, was on baby patrol. Now *there* was some irony.

He got into the truck and started it, the smooth purr of the motor belying the battered exterior, exactly the reason he'd wanted it. He, the guy who'd worked so hard at not doing what his father had done, leaving a string of bastards across the country, was now trying to earn his way out of prison and a felony record by helping some über-secret government agency crack, of all things, a baby-smuggling ring.

If they'd purposely searched out someone less suited, they couldn't have found him, Ryder had thought when they'd first approached him. Not only had he never had anything to do with babies, his life experience didn't include any knowledge whatsoever of what it would be like for a loving parent to lose a child. He'd never known anyone like that.

Well, Georgie. He had to admit that his sister obviously loved little Emmie. But he couldn't help thinking that was because she'd had the same experience he had, and was trying to make up for it. Or maybe she loved Emmie like she loved her horses, only...more. Maybe that was what it was like.

God, he was going slowly insane. He'd laugh if he weren't so tired. And bored.

He drove carefully—and as quickly as possible—through Esperanza, on his way back to San Antonio, where he was staying. He hadn't wanted to take the chance that someone in Esperanza might recognize him. While he looked a little different now—his hair was shorter and he'd filled out a bit—he'd been too well known, even notorious he supposed, in this little town to skate by unrecognized. It was much safer to lose himself among the million-plus population of the second largest city in the state.

The thought of doing it for real, taking this chance and just losing himself, dumping this crazy assignment he'd taken and making a break for it, starting over somewhere else, occurred to him, and not for the first time. East, to New York and the big city? Hell, he could lose himself forever there. Or L.A., maybe, warm, and thankfully dry weather, the beaches, paradise, right? He could lose himself there, too.

You can lose yourself anywhere. It's finding yourself that takes effort. You throw yourself away often enough, and one day you don't get it back.

Boots hadn't been talking about New York or L.A., but his words echoed in Ryder's head all the same. He didn't think he'd forgotten one single thing the older man had ever told him.

He'd thought at the time that it was just typical of his misbegotten life that he'd find the first human being who really gave a damn about him—the real him, not the impossible ideal Clay had always expected him to live up to—in a place like the Lone Star Correctional Facility. And that it would be a reformed armed robber who'd drawn the max because two people had died as a result of his crimes.

But regardless of all that, for the first time in his life, he started to see the way he was living it as a waste. He'd never worried about that before, rarely thought about it, but somehow Boots made him care. Made him want to change, to try another way.

He'd just never figured it would be such damn hard work. And he wasn't thinking about the job he'd taken on. That was the easy part.

He shook his head wearily, and drove on into the rising sun.

Ana Morales stood on the front porch of Jewel Mayfair's precious Hopechest Ranch house. She rubbed at her aching back with one hand as she gazed out over the ranchland bathed in the morning sun. To the east was San Antonio, she knew, although she had not ventured into that city the whole time she had been here. She could not risk it.

To the north was the vast, rolling, beautiful hill country of Texas. She would like to see it someday; she had heard so much chatter about everything from inner-tubing down the Guadalupe River to Saturday nights at the state's oldest honky-tonk. She smiled with a linguist's pleasure at the word; and Americans thought Spanish was odd!

Her pleasure at the word faded as she wondered if she would ever get to explore her love of languages again. Becoming a teacher had been her dream since childhood...and now here she was, nearly ready to bring a child into the world herself.

And by herself.

She turned to go back inside, back to the room Jewel had given her, no questions asked, at Ana's request; the room that looked out onto this porch—and gave the occupant a chance to see anyone who arrived. Before being seen herself.

She had been useful here. She had found purpose, something to focus on as she waited for the precious life within her to come into the world. And she had found someone else to worry about, she admitted; Jewel had been kindness personified to her, but Ana knew Jewel was deeply troubled. Too often, when Ana got up in the nighttime hours, suffering from the inability to find a comfortable position for her expanded body, she would find Jewel already up and walking the house. Sometimes Jewel had clearly been up for a while, sometimes she had the slightly wide-eyed look that told Ana she had been jolted awake by one of her nightmares.

It was those times that Ana felt rather small; this woman, who was working so hard here to provide the hope of the ranch's name to troubled kids, had had so much tragedy in her life. And yet she found solace in her work here—although not peace.

Or sleep.

Ana instinctively smoothed a hand protectively over the mound of her belly; she could not begin to imagine the horror of losing this child before it had a chance to live, as Jewel had lost hers. This life within her had been the impetus for everything she had done in the past seven months, since the day she had first suspected that she was pregnant.

"Getting heavy, that little one?"

Ana whirled around as quickly as she could, given her current bulk, chastising herself for getting so lost in her thoughts that she was caught off guard. That Jewel sometimes moved like a wraith around this place was no excuse in her mind.

"Sorry, I didn't mean to startle you."

"It is all right," Ana assured her. "I was actually just thinking about you. Did you finally get to sleep last night?"

"Some," Jewel said, but her weary brown eyes beneath the tousled cap of golden-brown hair told Ana that "some" had not been enough.

Doctor, heal thyself, Ana thought, although strictly speaking she knew Jewel was a psychologist, not a physician.

"Is there any more word?" Ana asked, turning to the subject that concerned her most; the very thought that a baby-smuggling ring was operating in the area terrified her. More than once she had thought she should move on, take her unborn child to a safer place, but she knew the folly of that; she had found shelter here, in a climate where most looked upon her as an enemy, just another illegal come to milk the American system. Of course, she was nothing of the kind.

She was secure here at the Hopechest Ranch, and it was simply up to her to keep her baby safe.

"Not that I've heard," Jewel answered. "But Adam will probably stop by later, and then I'll know for sure."

Ana smiled at the woman seventeen years her senior, and painfully wiser. "He is visiting more and more, Deputy Rawlings."

At first the sheriff's deputy had made Ana nervous, given her shaky immigration status. But the tall, strong man with the perfectly groomed dark hair and the always razor-creased uniform seemed only to have eyes for Jewel, which suited Ana just fine. Jewel deserved some happiness and his attention provided her benefactor—and herself, she admitted—with firsthand information on the ongoing investigation.

Jewel smiled, but absently. "Yes, he is."

"You do not like him?"

"Of course I do. He's been very kind to me."

"But…?"

"I'm not ready for that."

She didn't clarify, and Ana didn't ask. She had her own problems and wasn't about to counsel anyone in an area where she had made so many mistakes herself. She had trusted where she shouldn't have, and now she was paying the price. That one of the men she had trusted had been her own father didn't absolve her. Once she had found the evidence of his true character, it seemed the signs had been so clear she couldn't forgive herself for having missed them.

As for Alberto…she could not forgive herself for that, either. Yes, he was smooth, convincing, but so was her father.

Her baby kicked, mightily, as if the thoughts of traitorous men were unsettling to more than just her. She smiled as she put a hand over the spot.

"Kicking?" Jewel asked.

"Yes," Ana said, her smile widening. And then, suddenly remembering, her smile vanished. "Oh, Jewel, I am so sorry. It must be terribly hard for you to have me here, to see me, with my baby."

Jewel waved her to silence. "It's all right, Ana. I will never get over the loss of my baby, but I don't expect the world to stop turning and other women lucky enough to be pregnant to hide, just to spare my feelings."

Ana studied the benefactor who was rapidly becoming a friend. "You are very wise," she said.

"What I am," Jewel said frankly, "is very tired."

"I know," Ana said. "Is there anything I can do for you? Something else I can take over, so you can rest? Perhaps you might have better luck sleeping in the daytime?"

If Jewel was offended at the suggestion, or bothered by Ana's knowledge of her sleepless nights, she didn't let it show.

"I'll let you know. Thank you." A smile flashed across Jewel's face. "Unless you want to go riding with the older girls over at the Bar None this afternoon. I'm sure Clay can find a nice, gentle horse for you. You haven't left the ranch since you got here."

Ana was sure by Jewel's laugh that her fear must have shown in her face.

"Even if I could get this—" she gestured at her own bulk "—into a saddle, I wouldn't. Horses and I…no."

"You're in Texas now, girl. Better learn to love them."

"I do," Ana said. "They're beautiful creatures. But I prefer to admire them from a distance."

"You'll get over it," Jewel predicted. "It's in the water. And soon," Jewel warned her with a smile, "I'm going to make you take a break and have some fun."

Ana retreated to her room after that, wondering if the word *fun* would ever again be in her lexicon. It seemed a very, very long time since she had done anything but worry and plan and pray.

She stretched, trying to ease her aching back. If Jewel wouldn't take her advice about a nap this afternoon, perhaps she herself would. Along about three she was usually beginning to feel the strain of the extra weight she was carrying. Her feet would swell, her back would throb, and there would be nothing more welcome than to lie down for a while.

Except then there would be no distraction, nothing to keep her from dwelling on the unpleasant facts of her situation. She was twenty-two, unmarried and not likely to marry. She was about to become a mother, with a past in shambles behind her. But she was determined to build a life for herself and her baby.

She had never felt more alone.

And then the baby moved again. Ana set her jaw and her courage.

She was not alone. She had a tiny, helpless human being depending on her. A child she already loved beyond measure. She would make sure that child had a chance.

She would do whatever she had to to make that happen.

Chapter 2

By the time he reached his small, nondescript motel room, Ryder was feeling the too-familiar sensation of physical weariness coupled with being mentally amped up. It would be another day of restless sleep. He was definitely a night owl and used to sleeping in daylight—that was, according to Clay, one of his biggest failings—but doing nothing made him crazy.

"Buenos dias, mijo."

With his key—no modern card key for this old place—still in the door to his room, he looked over his shoulder to see the source of the "Good morning." It was Elena Sanchez, the tiny, round woman who ran this place with her husband, Julio. They'd been married, she had told Ryder at one point, nearly fifty years. The concept of being with one person that long boggled him.

"Hola, mamacita," he said, teasing her about her

tendency to mother him, even though she'd only known him a week. She also had amenably adapted her cleaning schedule to his, so that she never disturbed him when he was trying to sleep, but his room was always scrupulously clean; he appreciated that.

"You have been out all night again," she said.

"Working," he told her; something about the woman and her easy concern for a stranger made him want to reassure her.

Yeah. Like she'd be really reassured, considering how she feels family is everything, knowing you were out spying on your own brother's ranch. Better yet, tell her you're doing it because it got you out of prison, that ought to stop her worrying in a hurry.

"Have you eaten yet?"

"I just got here," he explained.

"Then you come eat with us. There is plenty."

"Thank you, but—" He stopped as she waved him to silence. And realized with a little jolt that he *liked* her worrying about him. That revelation put him off his game, and she won.

"You must eat," she said briskly, and bustled off, leaving him shaking his head at how neatly she'd trapped him. There was no way for him not to join the couple at their breakfast table yet again without being, in Elena's eyes, unforgivably rude.

And when the hell did you start worrying about being rude? he asked himself.

He supposed he could chalk that up to Boots, too. For all his rough edges, the man worked hard at doing what he'd never been able to do on the outside—be a decent human being. And that had included befriending a wild, out-of-control kid who'd landed in the adjoining cell.

Ryder's idea of learning hadn't included Boots's lectures, but with him in the next cell, he hadn't been able to avoid hearing the man. He'd taken to working on his collection of prison-style weapons. This, at least, he saw the need for; the looks and youth that had been a benefit on the outside earned him attention he could do without in prison. He learned fast, and was starting with a shiv made out of a toothbrush handle, since he wasn't allowed a belt with a buckle to hone to an edge. The work helped him tune out Boots's seemingly endless supply of reasons to turn his life around.

And that had included, later, convincing him to take the chance he'd been offered to clear his record and get out of prison before he was hardened beyond redemption.

A chance to do something good with his life.

A chance to help put away some guys doing some very nasty things.

A chance that had ended up with him coming full circle, back to Esperanza, where he'd grown up and gotten into trouble in the first place.

A chance that landed him, after following a trail that led all over the Southwest, where he was now. Spying on the Bar None ranch.

Home.

Not that he'd ever felt that way. All he'd ever felt at the Bar None was out of place. And a disappointment to his big brother. His little sister had been better; she had enough fire in her to understand Ryder's restlessness.

And look where that got her, he told himself. With a kid at eighteen, after she fell for some handsome, sweet-talking city dude. He'd have thought his sassy little sister would have been too smart for that, but some women were just suckers for a pretty face.

Lucky for you, he thought with a wry grimace, knowing that, except for the city part, he could have been talking about himself. He'd loved—well, in the here today, gone tomorrow sense—and left more than one woman, although after Georgie had turned up pregnant at eighteen he'd taken the lesson to heart and been very, very careful. Up until then he figured if a pregnancy ever happened he'd do just what his father had done—have nothing to do with it.

But after seeing what Georgie, the one sibling he could almost relate to, had gone through, the last thing he ever wanted was a baby to muck up the works, so he'd taken every precaution. His plan from early on had been to have as much fun as he could for as long as he lived, and that included taking advantage of how much women were attracted to him. That they weren't the kind of women who stayed didn't matter; he wasn't that kind of man, either.

"You are quiet this morning, *chico,*" Julio said after they'd eaten, one of Elena's usual vast spreads of eggs, beans, and fresh tortillas made and patted out by her own hands.

Ryder wasn't sure how to respond. "I say fewer stupid things that way," he finally answered.

That earned him a smile from the usually taciturn Mr. Sanchez. "More should do as you do."

By way of thank you—and habit; there had been no one to clean up after them in their house, whether they were Gradys or Coltons—he helped clear the table. And he *was* thankful; the full, warm meal might help him actually get some sleep before he had to start in again.

Back in his small but clean and tidy room, Ryder took a quick shower, wrapped a towel around his waist and sat on the edge of the bed. He reached into the nightstand drawer and took out his pay-as-you-go cell phone. He had the other one, the one they'd given him to use, the one they paid the bill on. But there were some things Ryder preferred to keep private, and his talks with Boots definitely fell into that category, for both their sakes. The convict had gruffly made him promise to stay in touch, which, according to him, meant to take the weekly call Boots made.

That was a lot more staying in touch than Ryder was used to, but he hadn't been able to say no to the older man. Not after everything he'd done. So for the past seven months, when the phone rang on Wednesday mornings, he answered it.

Right on cue, the cell rang.

"How goes it, boy?"

"Not backward," Ryder said dryly.

Boots chuckled, that raspy, wry sound Ryder always associated with the older man. He could picture him, on the phone in the dayroom, lean, wiry and leathery. After fifteen years in prison, his ability to laugh at all was a marvel. Ryder thought his own three years had leached all humor out of him, and left him with only that new appreciation of irony.

"Sometimes," Boots said, "that's the best you can hope for."

"It's not enough."

"Depends on who's doing the grading. You always did want more faster."

Boots didn't point out that that very trait had been what had landed Ryder in trouble so many times—okay, most times—in his life. Perhaps he assumed it was obvious, even to Ryder, that he didn't have to.

Perhaps it was that obvious. Ryder jammed a hand through his thick, dark, and still shower-damp hair.

"So no progress?"

"I'm running out of cigars," Ryder said. "Is that progress?"

"Of a sort," Boots said with another chuckle.

Ryder had to consider his words carefully. After all, he wasn't supposed to be discussing his new "job" with anyone. But since Boots already knew about it—he'd been with Ryder when the men in the dark suits and the government-issue sunglasses had shown up in the first place—Ryder didn't figure he was giving away any state secrets talking to him, as long as he was careful.

"It's strange. To be out there, but…not to be. To have to hide."

He'd managed to let Boots know how the trail he'd been following had led him to, of all places, his brother's Bar None ranch.

"You don't think he's involved, do you?"

At the very thought of straight-arrow Clay being involved in anything illicit, Ryder had to smother a laugh. "No way in hell," he said succinctly. "I'm the problem child in that family."

"Were," Boots said gently.

"You'd be hard-pressed to convince my brother of that, I'm guessing."

"I won't have to," Boots said. "You will. Once you're free of all this."

This was old ground; Boots was determined that Ryder would reunite with his family, once this was all over. Ryder had tried to tell him Clay had washed his hands of him, and once Clay made up his mind, it took heaven and earth to change it. While Ryder believed in earth—at least the six feet of it he expected to be under before he was forty—heaven? No.

Somewhat to his surprise, Boots, a deeply religious man now, didn't push it on him. He believed enough for both of them.

"I've got to get some sleep, if I'm going to go out and play spy again tonight."

"You're not playing," Boots reminded him. "If this is for real, it could be dangerous."

Ryder couldn't quite imagine baby smugglers as armed and threatening.

As if he'd read his thoughts—Boots was good at that, even over the phone—the man chided him gently. "You're not taking this seriously enough, Ryder. Don't let the nature of the contraband fool you. There's a lot of money at stake in this venture. Probably more per ounce than any you'll ever come across."

He'd never thought of it that way. He really had no idea how much it cost to buy a kid, and he hadn't asked. Maybe he should. Because Boots was right; where there was money, there were men who would fight to get it and keep it.

"Something's coming," Boots said. "You watch your back."

"You been talking to the Boss again?" Ryder teased; Boots spoke to God as if he were a poker buddy sometimes, making what he called "suggestions," most of which of late seemed to involve the salvation of one Ryder Colton. And no matter how much Ryder tried to talk the old man out of it, Boots never gave up on him.

More than I can say for my brother, he thought as Boots ignored the jibe.

"More the other way around. Just a feeling, Ryder. Be watchful."

With that Boots's phone time was up, and the call ended.

That was what drove him craziest about Boots and his beliefs, Ryder thought; no matter what happened later, the man would nod wisely and say, "I told you." If what happened was something good, it was straight from his

God. If it was something bad, God's intervention had lessened the blow.

Yet, Ryder thought as he pulled the thankfully room-darkening curtains of the small motel room closed, he couldn't deny that the man's pure, shining faith had had an effect on him. He'd fought it, resisted fiercely, but Boots's quiet determination to save him from himself had made inroads.

He'd finally decided that the principles underlying Boots's beliefs were good no matter what the foundation. And when Boots had laughed and told him he didn't have to believe to live by them, the result was the same—Ryder had felt a sudden sense of relief he'd never known before. And in that moment he'd determined to give it a shot, for the sake of the man who had seen something in him worth saving, a man who would never see the outside again, but still found hope.

To his surprise he slept well, for nearly seven hours. More than enough to keep going. He got up, dressed, grabbed his last box of Little Travis cigars and headed out. He wasn't hungry yet; Mrs. Sanchez's hearty breakfast was still holding. So he headed instead to the local library branch.

It wasn't as foreign territory to him as he supposed many might think, given his capacity for trouble. There had been times when he'd wanted information, and had wanted to get it without his big brother hanging over his shoulder. Esperanza's tiny library was just that, tiny, and his presence would be noticed—and reported on to Clay within hours—so he'd avoided that. But there were other towns, other libraries, and he spread it around.

His official cell phone rang as he pulled into the parking lot of the library.

"You didn't check in," a stern voice said.

"I did," Ryder countered. "I left a message. Not my fault you didn't answer. I needed sleep."

His alternate handler—an agent named Gibson—apparently decided to let it go. "Developments?"

I'm about out of cigars and my ass is tired of sitting all night in the dark, waiting for nothing, he thought. But he knew better than to bitch, at this guy in particular. He was a little more human, and sometimes even unbent enough to commiserate with the frustration Ryder felt. Ryder didn't want to blow that.

"Nothing. No movement, no sign of movement, and nobody who shouldn't be around. They go lights out around here early, and it stays that way."

Work started very early on a ranch, and Clay Colton was serious about work. Ryder had chosen to ignore his brother's work ethic and this had always been the biggest bone of contention between the two brothers.

That, and the fact that Ryder had been born for trouble.

"The biggest thing that's happened around here is people keep getting married," Ryder said. "The sheriff, his brother..."

Ryder clammed up before he let slip something that gave him away. It wouldn't do to mention that he knew his ex-sister-in-law was back on the ranch, or the even bigger shock of learning that his little sister had married some overtense suit.

As far as his handlers knew, he had no family. None of them really wanted to claim him, so he'd done the same. On anything that had required listing next of kin, he'd put "None." And that's how it would stay. For all he knew, that's why they'd picked him for this job. Maybe Boots was right, and this was more potentially dangerous than he'd realized.

Not that it mattered. He could get blown away tomorrow, and it would barely cause a ripple. Boots might shake his head sadly, but that was the truth. No one else would really care. Not that he expected them to; there was something inherently wrong with him. If even his own father and brother wanted nothing to do with him, why would anyone else?

"We need to get this wrapped up," Gibson said. "The Colton campaign is on its way to San Antonio soon, and we do not want to try and run this operation with all that going on."

The casual reference gave Ryder a jolt. He'd been so focused on his little bit of work here, the bigger happenings in the world hadn't even registered. Not that he ever paid much attention to politics, not even presidential politics.

He wondered what that cool, commanding voice on the other end of the phone would think if he realized that he was speaking to a man who was, technically if not officially, the nephew of the man who could well become president of the United States.

Wasn't there some branch of the feds who investigated all the family members of people who aspired to the highest office? It only made sense. And the fact that Joe Colton's ne'er-do-well brother had fathered a crop of kids outside his marriage wasn't exactly a secret.

For the first time, it hit Ryder that he was, by blood, connected to a very famous family. Not that they would claim him any more than his own father had, but still, if he were mercenary enough…

He could almost see Boots's frown. Could hear the old man's stern warning that that way lay hellfire. Could even hear himself answering, "Don't worry, Boots. That'd mean I'd have to claim Graham Colton as my father, and that ain't ever going to happen."

That much was the truth. No amount of money or

famous family would make him do that. He might feel a bit of wistful sadness about losing his brother and sister—they'd once been a tight-knit group—but his father meant less than nothing to him.

As he meant less than nothing to his father.

"Don't forget to check in when you're in place tonight."

"Yeah," Ryder said absently, locking the truck as he headed for the library. He could have asked how much money they were talking about here, but caution won out; he didn't want them thinking he was pondering going over to the other side.

He didn't think his recruiters had believed him when he'd told them, just as he had told the court at his trial, that he'd never intended to smuggle illegals into the country. That he'd merely been paid to drive a truck, that as far as he knew was full of computer equipment. No one had believed him back then.

In fact, it had barely bothered him that he'd ended up in prison for something he hadn't intended to do. As he'd told Boots later, when the man had begun to talk to him about his future, he'd done enough intentionally to land him here anyway.

"It's just karma catching up with me," he'd said. "No big deal."

"But a big chance," Boots had said, already launching into his crusade to salvage Ryder's life.

Ryder hadn't been listening to the older man, though. Not then. This situation wasn't going to change anything, not really. To his way of thinking, it was just a speed bump on his racetrack, and he'd be back at full tilt as soon as he got out. Older and wiser, maybe. Hopefully wise enough to keep from getting caught next time trouble irresistibly called his name.

Once he'd spent a couple of hours in the library researching, he was a little stunned at what he'd found. At how much people would pay for a child they knew nothing about. At how long this had been going on, seemingly forever. At how many ways it happened, from the simple theft straight out of a hospital nursery, to unethical doctors who arranged black market adoptions, to unscrupulous lawyers who facilitated all of it.

He was stunned most of all at the fierce desire for a baby that drove it all.

He headed back out to the ranch to start another evening of surveillance and endless waiting. He made his usual circuit to check the tunnels suspected of being used by the ring, but his telltales—small things he'd placed that would be pushed aside or stepped on unknowingly by anyone who went through the openings—were undisturbed, as they had been for days now. This obviously wasn't a high-volume operation.

Or he was on the wrong track altogether, which he didn't like contemplating.

When he was done with his inspections, he settled in in a key spot and waited for full dark before moving in closer to the ranch.

Once more, Ryder found himself sitting and watching, with nothing to do but think. He tried all sorts of distractions, from taking Boots's theory and trying to figure in his head what a six-pound baby would cost per ounce at the going rate, to deciding what approach to use on that cute waitress at the diner down the street from the motel. Nothing seemed to work very well. And he kept coming back full circle, thinking about the family who'd cut him off.

Although, to be fair, he'd done the same thing.

Was he luckier to *know* his family? Luckier than a kid

who'd been sold, but at least to people who wanted him? Or worse, stolen, maybe from a parent who actually loved him? He wasn't sure.

As darkness fell around him again, Ryder worked his way slowly down toward the new building that had been put up since he'd been gone, the building he suspected might be a stop on the smugglers' route. How different his life might have been if he'd been stolen as a baby. Better? Maybe. Easier? Probably.

But then he felt a jab of guilt. Clay had sacrificed a great deal, trying to keep them all together. Ryder hadn't ever wanted to admit that, but he couldn't deny it any longer. Clay had tried harder than anyone had any right to expect. It wasn't his fault that his little brother was a screwed-up mess. But knowing Clay, he probably blamed himself. Ryder grimaced inwardly.

The only language you seem to understand is trouble. And when it calls, you come running.

No sooner had the words formed in his mind than he heard it. A low, agonized whimper of sound.

He froze. Instantly his brain discarded the possibility that it had been a baby's cry; this was someone older, an adult. He tilted his head, trying to triangulate the sound.

Inside the house.

It came again, harsher this time, a cry of pain and anguish that stabbed at him.

A woman. It was a woman.

Instinctively he took a step forward, then stopped himself.

The only language you understand is trouble. And when it calls, you come running....

His thoughts taunted him. Somewhere in the back of his mind a little voice told him to walk away, all the while laughing, knowing he wouldn't.

Knowing he couldn't.
Trouble was calling.
And, God help him, he was going to answer.

Chapter 3

Ana knew she was in trouble. Jewel had taken the Hopechest children into town for a treat, a movie and then ice cream at Miss Sue's. Although Jewel had asked her to accompany them, Ana's back had been aching fiercely all day. She had seized the chance for some quiet in the empty house; with Macy Ward, the recreational therapist at Hopechest, away on her honeymoon with the sheriff's brother, Fisher Yates, Hope chest was completely deserted—and peaceful—tonight.

She had dozed fitfully through the ache and awakened after an hour to the empty house. She had panicked, knowing now the reason her back had been aching so.

The baby.

When the first contraction ripped through her it caught her off guard and she screamed. The sound echoed off the walls of the deserted house, and she bit her lip in the effort to stop another cry.

As the pain ebbed, for a brief moment she allowed herself to hope it was only a false alarm. Surely she would not be so unlucky as to give birth at the worst possible moment, when she had no one here to help?

And why would this surprise you? she asked herself sternly. *Your judgment in life has been so sterling thus far.*

Slowly, she sat up, relieved when she was able to do so. Her water had broken, she couldn't deny that, but perhaps the baby would wait at least until Jewel returned. She thought about calling the Bar None, but she was certain Jewel had mentioned that Clay Colton was out with his ex-wife.

It seemed like an odd thing to her; she could no more imagine going back to Alberto Cardenas than she could imagine stopping this baby from coming. Not now that she knew he was as bad as her father. But she knew not everyone was as unlucky—or unwise—as she was.

On that thought, a second contraction hit, shocking another cry out of her. This time she had the presence of mind to look at the clock; timing was important, was it not?

Tears brimmed in her eyes and she told herself it was the pain. She would not cower and whine, she simply would not. Determined, she tried to stand. If she could walk, perhaps she could stave this off until help arrived.

Her first steps convinced her of the folly of that notion. She made it to the chest of drawers a few feet away before another pain struck, sending her to her knees; she barely managed to cling to the heavy piece of furniture and keep from falling.

In the process she pulled over the small statue of a roadrunner Jewel had so kindly given her when she had arrived here. She had seen it in the library and exclaimed that it reminded her of home. Thinking that Ana was homesick, Jewel had offered the piece. Ana had accepted it, temporarily, thinking it would serve as a good reminder of all the reasons why she had left.

The statue shattered on the tile floor, having just missed the colorful rug in front of the chest. Ana barely had time to regret the miscue before another pain hit. She did not have to look at the clock to know it was too soon; the pains were too close together to pretend.

Her baby was coming.

She was alone.

She was going to have to do this herself. Somehow.

And she would, she told herself fiercely. She'd gotten her baby into this, it was up to her to handle it. She—

Her self-lecture broke off at a sound from the porch. For an instant she felt relieved until she realized she had not heard the ranch van pulling up the driveway, or heard the door open to the garage, which was next to her room.

It was not Jewel.

It was not anyone who had arrived openly by car. And while it was possible, even a frequent occurrence, that a visitor would arrive on horseback, she had not heard that either. And at this hour of night, that did not seem likely.

No answer she could come up with was good.

A tall shadow shot across the tile floor, hiding the gleam of the broken pieces of the statue. Ana choked back the scream that rose to her throat. She grabbed the largest, sharpest shard of the shattered roadrunner. It was not much, but it was all she had to protect herself and her baby.

As the shadow moved closer and she found herself staring up into the eyes of a tall, dark, menacing stranger, she thought she was going to have to defend the two of them.

Trouble, he'd expected.

A very pregnant woman, he hadn't.

He'd done his homework on this place, this Hopechest Ranch. He'd been a little taken aback when he'd learned that the Hopechest Foundation that funded it was the pet project of Meredith Colton, who was his aunt. And potential first lady.

But he hadn't heard even a rumor that the place helped illegals. He considered the woman's obviously Hispanic appearance and wondered if she had run away from home. Everything he'd read had indicated the place was a home for troubled teens, not pregnant ones. Although maybe the two sometimes went hand in hand.

It occurred to him momentarily that he might well have been considered one of those teens not long ago. But he'd never thought of himself as "troubled," just determined to have fun. There'd been too little fun in his life, and he'd been set on making up for that.

And then it hit him. Was he perhaps closer than he'd realized to his goal? Had he inadvertently stumbled onto yet another aspect of the investigation, something they didn't even know?

Was this pregnant woman here not just to have her baby, but to get rid of it? Was it already bought and paid? She didn't look or act the type, but what did he know about that? Perhaps her protective posture was to save her investment, not her child.

The woman on her knees doubled over, and he heard the moan she tried to hold back. She was dressed in some flowing cotton gown in a pure white that gleamed in the moonlight. She was clutching something in her hand, something that looked like a piece of broken pottery. Suddenly she straightened slightly and waved it at him with an unsteady hand.

"*¡Salir de aqui!*" she said, her voice slightly steadier than her hand.

As she told him to get out of here, he realized she had some idea of using that little shard as a weapon. He nearly laughed aloud, but she was so clearly frightened he quashed the urge.

"No tengas miedo," he said, although he doubted that simply telling her not to be afraid would alleviate the problem. After all, from her point of view he'd turned up out of the dark, she was clearly alone, and in pain...

In labor.

Belatedly it hit him.

My God, she was having that baby now.

Even as he thought it she cried out again, hunching protectively over her swollen belly.

"Damn," he muttered. "You're going to have that thing right now, aren't you?"

"That *thing* is a baby!" she snapped in perfect English.

He held up his hands at the sudden fierceness of her tone. "Sorry," he said. "But I'm right, aren't I?"

"It is coming, yes," she said, and suddenly the fierceness vanished, replaced by an almost tangible fear. Ryder realized how young she was, even younger than he was. Twenty, maybe twenty-two?

"Now?"

He was more than a little scared himself. He didn't know a thing about this process, and at the moment wished he had stayed where he belonged, out there on that fruitless, useless stakeout.

"Right now," she said grimly, doubling over once more.

"Damn," he said again.

He bent to try to help her get up, but she pulled away from him. Instead she grabbed the edge of the heavy, carved chest beside her, and tried to pull herself to her feet. She fell back to her knees as another pain apparently hit.

Close together, those pains, he thought. That meant it really was imminent, didn't it? He'd seen movies, read stories…

But this was real life, about to happen right in front of him, and he was the only one here. No empathetic woman to take over. He should have paid more attention to his sister, but the very idea made him nervous and he'd avoided the subject entirely.

What if he called Georgie? Would she even talk to him? As far as his family knew, he was still in prison, he guessed. By now even Georgie, his sometimes partner in mischief as children, had probably washed her hands of him. She'd somehow turned very serious when she'd had a child to think about. Children really did change everything.

The woman moaned, shifting on the floor as if trying to escape the pain. The movement took her into the shaft of moonlight that came through the front window of the room. And he realized with a sudden jolt that she was lovely. Her long, dark hair fell in thick waves well past her shoulders. Her eyes were just as dark and caught the light enough to show him they were wide with pain and brimming with moisture.

She moaned again, and the helpless sound of it galvanized him. He didn't know if it was some instinctive male gene that drove him toward protecting a woman in her most helpless yet miraculous time. Or maybe something more personal. He only knew he couldn't just leave her like this. She needed help, and he was the only one around.

Unluckily for you, *chica,* he thought to himself.

He scooped her up off the floor. It was clumsy, because of her bulk and the effort not to hurt her any more, but once he had her he was a little surprised; he'd thought she would be heavier, what with the baby. It hit him that he was carrying one person back to the bed, but before long there would be two. The idea rocked him. He'd never been this close to a birth before.

"You must have done something to get ready for this," he said.

"There are...blankets and things...in the trunk." She made a gesture toward the heavy trunk at the foot of the bed. He went to it quickly, lifted the lid, found the things she'd mentioned. He got out the pile of soft cotton cloths, spotted a pair of scissors in a sealed package and grabbed those, too.

Cord, he thought. You had to cut the cord, right?

God, he was way out of his depth.

"There's no one to call?" he asked her, wanting to be absolutely certain before he committed to this.

"No one...could be here...in time."

She was panting now, and he wondered if she'd taken some class in special breathing—didn't they always say stuff about that?—or if it just happened naturally.

He laid her gently down on the bed. She cried out as another pain seized her. He reached over and turned on a bedside lamp, turned back and forgot to breathe for a moment.

She was more than pretty, she was beautiful. Her wide, dark eyes were huge, gleaming in the light. Her skin was a light, luscious olive tone—smooth, flawless, glowing. Her lips were full, soft, and slightly parted as she tried hard not to moan; he could see the ferocious effort she was making. It jogged him back to reality, and the urgent matter at hand.

"I don't know anything about this," he told her. "You'll have to tell me what to do."

"And you think...I know?" Her laugh wasn't bitter, but it wasn't amused, either. And for the first time he wondered how she'd gotten into this situation. He couldn't quite believe she'd done it intentionally, getting pregnant to sell the baby. It was feasible. But something in her dark, exotic eyes, and the way she looked up at him, made that impossible for him to believe, at least right now.

And it didn't really matter right now. Whether she was involved in the smuggling ring or not didn't change what was about to happen. Working on some combination of stories heard and movies seen, he did what seemed reasonable, starting with rolling up his sleeves and washing his hands in the bathroom just down the hall.

"How old are you?" he asked when he came back.

She looked startled, then wary.

"I'm only asking because my sister got pregnant four years ago. She was only eighteen."

The woman smothered another moan, then answered. "I am twenty-two."

Better, he guessed. But not much. "She fell for a smooth-talking city boy. He deserted her."

It wasn't a question, nor was there any emotion in the flat assertion.

"Is that what happened to you?" he asked softly. "He deserted you, when he found out you were pregnant?"

He found himself hoping she'd say yes, that she was here because she simply had no choice, not because she had the soul of a mercenary.

"No," she said, her tone still flat. "It was I…who ran."

Ryder blinked. He hadn't expected that.

A sharp cry broke from her, and he realized the pains were coming closer together, and even he knew what that meant. No more time to try and find out who this woman was or why she was here, what her motives were.

"Hot water," he muttered. They always talked about that, too, didn't they?

"No…time."

He realized she meant that literally.

"The baby…is coming."

Now. She meant right now.

Ryder stifled the urge to run. Her hands flailed wildly, as if seeking purchase. He grabbed them, startled at the strength in them as she cried out yet again.

"It's all right," he said, squeezing her hands. "We'll get through it." *Somehow,* he added silently to himself.

He had no plan; he worked strictly on instinct. He kept up a stream of encouraging words, trying to distract her—and perhaps himself—from the embarrassingly intimate position they found themselves in. He wasn't sure it helped, but when he paused she asked him to keep talking.

Until it started to actually happen.

He'd had no idea birth was such a messy thing. He'd always had some image that the kid slid out and got wrapped in a blanket and handed over. But this was wet, bloody and shockingly brutal. He didn't know who to marvel at more—the woman going through it, or the child for surviving it.

If, of course, it did.

It was when he first spotted the baby's head emerging that his gut truly knotted. Dark hair, nearly as dark as his own. He was a little startled. He thought babies were born bald.

The woman screamed then. It was a rending sound, and he touched her gently, trying to soothe her.

"It's coming," he said, even though he realized that no one knew that better just now than she did. "It'll be over soon."

She seemed to take heart from that, and sucked in a breath.

"Can you push?" he asked diffidently, wondering if that was just a stupid cliché, too.

She grunted then, a primal, earthy sound. Then again, and again.

Women, he thought. You heard about what they went through in childbirth, but until you saw it, you didn't really realize how tough they were.

To Ryder, it seemed to happen fast then, although he suspected it wouldn't be wise to say so to the straining woman. He should be paying more attention to the baby, and shifted just in time to see a tiny pair of shoulders emerge.

It did happen fast then. He reached to support the tiny thing she was expelling.

The moment he touched it, the "thing" became real to him. He stared down at the baby who barely filled his two hands. So tiny, so helpless…but it was a life, another human being, a fellow inhabitant of this glorious planet, and he'd helped it arrive.

This was big, he thought.

Huge.

How could something so incredibly small, so fragile and delicate, make him feel like this?

"It's a girl," he whispered. "A little girl."

The woman made a sound he couldn't begin to describe. She sounded exhausted, but there was something else in her voice when she instructed, "You must cut the cord."

He winced, even though he knew that. He followed her brisk instructions, glad she was able to walk him through it. She might be young, but she'd clearly done her homework on this.

Or maybe women were just born knowing, he thought, despite her earlier claim to ignorance.

"I just leave it like that?" he asked, looking doubtfully at the stub of the cord still attached to the baby who appeared to be, to his amazement, looking around. Her eyes were brown, he thought, a little numbly. Dark, rich, espresso brown, like her mother's. Her head looked a little funny, misshapen, but he guessed that was normal.

"It will fall off of its own accord later," the woman said. "You must clean her. Her mouth, nose, so that she breathes easily."

He did his best, aware that he was shaking slightly. And when the tiny child in his hands let out a protesting wail, he found himself grinning; things were working fine, it seemed.

"She's got lungs," he said, feeling a bit loopy, as if he'd downed one tequila too many. To his surprise the new mother laughed, as if she hadn't just been through hell.

When she was clean and dry, he wrapped the baby awkwardly, but with a need for gentleness unlike anything he'd ever felt before. He took a last look down into the tiny face.

"Give her to me."

The new mother's voice was shaky, and when he looked from daughter to mother he saw fear in her eyes. She reached out, as if she were afraid he would refuse to hand over the baby. Ryder wondered suddenly if she knew what was going on around here, and had the sudden thought that she might suspect him of being connected to the baby-smuggling ring.

Well, she's right, isn't she? he told himself.

Then he put the baby into her mother's outstretched arms. The look that mother gave him nearly stopped his heart cold.

"Thank you," she whispered.

For the first time in his life with a woman, Ryder was speechless. All he could do was look at her, and at the tiny bit of humanity he'd just helped bring into the world. He didn't know how he felt, only that whatever it was, it was more intense than he'd ever experienced before.

And on some level, somewhere deep inside him, he knew he would never be the same again.

Chapter 4

Maria.

Ana held her baby close, savoring the feel of her, the smell of her, the miracle of her.

She had thought of other names, but when the time had come there was no other. Maria. Her mother deserved the tribute; it was not her fault that Ana's father had not been the man she had hoped. For a long time, Ana was grateful her mother had died before she'd learned the full extent of her husband's dishonesty and evil. But now, she could only feel sad that her mother was not here to see this precious child, her granddaughter.

So she would do the only thing she could; she would name her after her grandmother and give her the life she deserved. Somehow, she would do this. She would ask for no help, no charity, she would make her own way, for herself and her baby girl.

No help…

"A hospital," the dark stranger said. "You and she need to see a doctor."

Ana shook her head. She trusted no one, especially now. She had heard too much about the local baby smuggling, had pumped Jewel daily for information, information she'd given sometimes reluctantly, for fear of frightening the soon-to-be mother.

"I am not going anywhere."

"But what if there's something wrong?"

"There is nothing wrong. She is beautiful. Healthy. You can see that."

"But what about you? That was…you need—"

"No." It sounded cold and heartless to her ears, when all he'd done was express concern about her. She hastened to add, "I—and my daughter—thank you for what you did. But you must go now."

He looked nonplussed. She supposed it was rude, but what did rudeness matter when she had her baby to protect? She knew Jewel would be back with the kids soon, then she would have help she trusted.

She did not, could not dare trust this man. She didn't know why he was here, how he had happened to arrive just as she needed help. For all she knew, he was one of them, had been watching her, a pregnant woman obviously alone, thinking perhaps to steal her baby as so many others had been stolen, ripped from the loving arms of their mothers and sold as if they were packages of cereal.

"You don't trust me, do you?" he said softly.

"I do not trust anyone," she said. "A lesson I should have learned earlier."

He studied her for a moment, and then, to her surprise, nodded. "Wise choice."

His voice was soft, gentle, but it held a harsh undertone that stirred something in her. Who was this man who had strode in out of the moonlight and helped her without questions? What had he been—what had he done—to sound like that? Was he truly one of them? Was her baby still in danger from him?

"Go," she said, her voice sharp as her fears grew in proportion to the exhaustion that was growing, threatening to overwhelm her at any moment.

"I can't just leave you here alone."

"I will not be alone for long. People will be back here soon."

"You don't have to lie to get me to leave."

"I am not lying. The woman who runs this place, she will be back with her charges soon. They only went to town for an outing."

He lifted a brow at her, and she wondered what she'd said. Her English was, she knew, nearly perfect. She'd worked hard at that in college, intending to put it to use teaching in a bilingual school.

But sometimes, she realized it was too perfect; local idioms and slang peppered the talk of others, but her college-taught skills stood out, marked her as different. But she'd long ago decided she would rather be different that way; if she was going to be judged, as people were, by the way she spoke, better too well than not well enough. That had always been her way. She saw no reason to change it now.

"Go. Please."

He hesitated a moment longer, looking down at her. He towered over the bed, so tall, long-legged and strong, she thought. His eyes were dark, piercing, and she couldn't help feeling he saw more than she wished. His jaw was stubbled with slight beard growth, as if he hadn't shaved since this morning. His hair was even darker than her own, and fell in a silky if shaggy sweep over his brow when he leaned forward. She wanted to run her fingers through it and push it back.

That thought sent a stab of shock and fear through her. She needed this man gone. She obviously was not thinking clearly in the aftermath of this life-changing experience. The very last thing she should be doing at this moment was finding a man attractive. Especially a man she knew absolutely nothing about.

Of course, she had thought she knew everything about Alberto as well.

"Go," she said again. "Please."

"You swear to me that there will be help here soon?"

His concern moved her against her will. "I swear. And I repeat, I do not lie."

She meant that. Small, kind lies to avoid hurt feelings were one thing, although she preferred to avoid those as well. But big lies about things that mattered had shaped then destroyed her world. She hated them.

For another silent moment, her rescuer, the man who had helped deliver the baby squirming in her arms, stared down at her. And then, sharply, he nodded.

"Be well," he said, in a tone she couldn't describe, some combination of command, awe and benediction. She had the oddest thought that this time had been life-changing for more than just herself. But this handsome American seemed too strong to let something affect him that much.

And then he was gone, disappearing back into the darkness as silently as he'd appeared, surprising her that a man of his size could move so quietly. It was unsettling, someone that big should make more noise, she thought. And in her exhaustion her imagination began to come up with reasons why a man like that would learn to move so stealthily—and none of them were good.

She was relieved that he had gone. She had half expected him to grab her baby out of her arms, proving himself part of the ring she so feared and that the local authorities were so diligently searching for.

But she could not deny he'd been a godsend. She did not want to think about what she would have done had he not appeared out of the darkness.

But she also did not want to think about what she would have done had he refused to go back into that darkness.

She cuddled her baby close, running through her mind all that she had studied: when to feed her, how she would know when she herself was ready for that, all the things she'd so voraciously read in preparation for this day. The pain she'd just endured was nearly forgotten already, although the gentle, encouraging touch and words of the dark stranger were not. She thought she would never forget those, or him. One day it might be a fascinating story to tell her daughter, about the unknown man who had come to their aid, and then vanished into the night.

Perhaps in time she would wonder if he had even been real, that tall, dark man. She smiled at her own silliness, a little surprised that she was still capable of such fantasy. Perhaps she was already preparing stories to tell her child at bedtime.

Instinctively she began to sing quietly to Maria, a sweet little lullaby her mother had sung to her.

Duérmete mi niña,

Duérmete mi sol...

Not that she actually wanted her little sunshine to sleep just yet, she was still too caught up in the wonder of it all. At last, she held this miracle in her arms, and she felt she must do something motherly, something to show this tiny human being she was loved and welcomed, even if she was lacking one of her parents.

"Better no father than an evil one, *mija,*" she whispered, determined that the baby would hear English as much as Spanish as she grew and learned to speak.

Yes, it would be different for Maria. She would grow up speaking both, at home in both tongues in a way her mother would never be. But it was what she'd wanted, Ana told herself. She was alone, isolated by choice from the family she'd once been close to. The family she'd once trusted.

You must remember who they really are, she told herself. She couldn't help thinking some of them had to know what she had only recently learned, how vast were the criminal dealings her father was involved in. Once she herself had found out, the evidence was so obvious she could not believe she had missed it for so long. The older ones, her father's brothers, sisters, the ones she could no longer think of as aunts and uncles, they must have known.

Had they indeed known, and conspired to keep it from her? Or had no conspiracy been necessary? Was she such a naïve fool that they had managed to keep the truth from her with no such effort?

The baby stilled, seemingly calmed by the sweet song. Ana held her even closer. She closed her eyes, shifting in the bed. The big man had seen to her comfort in an unexpectedly gentle manner, cleaning her, changing the bedclothes, and disposing of the mess of the birth quickly and efficiently. For a man who claimed to know nothing about the process, she thought he had handled it with remarkable aplomb. Her mother had often told her how her own father had been worse than useless. She liked the idea that her gallant stranger was much more of a man than her wicked father. She wondered what that stranger was thinking now, if he'd already put them out of his mind, if what had been a miracle to her was simply an odd occurrence to him.

He probably thinks you're just another illegal looking for a handout, she thought.

She told herself it didn't matter what he thought, not when she herself knew the truth. She was an intelligent woman, she had an education to offer, and she was going to start a new life for herself and her daughter. She would do it herself, without charity or handouts. Anything given to her, she would repay, in some form, as she was helping here at Hopechest Ranch in return for Jewel's hospitality and kindness.

No matter what it took, she and Maria would make their way, and have a good life.

"I promise you, *mijita.* You will be safe, you will have good things, you will grow and learn, and above all else you will be loved."

Ana settled in to wait, wondering what Jewel would think when she returned to find the population of her beloved Hopechest Ranch increased by one.

Chapter 5

This was insane, Ryder thought a couple nights later.

There was no reason in hell why that woman and her baby should haunt him like this.

He'd done the right thing. He might be the black sheep of the Texas Coltons, but even he had been unable to simply leave a pregnant woman in labor without help.

So why couldn't he just chalk it up to some unexpected sense of decency, hope it might someday tip the judgment scales in his favor and move on with the job he was here to do?

He shook his head as he drove to a meeting with Alcazar. A daylight meeting for a change, which Ryder acknowledged with wry humor; rats didn't usually come out in the sunlight.

And he himself was tired, tired enough that he needed to be on guard against making a mistake. His time in prison had given him some creds with the gang he hadn't had before. He'd had to spin a tale about how he'd been released early due to prison overcrowding and good behavior—a first in his lifetime, he'd laughed as he relayed the carefully concocted story—and Alcazar had obviously checked it out before setting up this meeting today.

Ironically, the track his investigation had led him on, all around New Mexico and southwest Texas, had served to cement his position. He'd done a few jobs for people Alcazar knew, and word had gotten back.

Of course, he'd had to cover his ass with his new, government bosses, and had reported on each incident. They'd told him going in that a lot would be forgiven if he accomplished the main goal. Apparently they'd meant it; nothing had come down on him for doing exactly what had landed him in custody in the first place, joining the coyotes who traveled under cover of darkness, smuggling in illegals.

Only this time, he was doing it with full intention and knowledge. It was still unsettling even though the feds had ordered him to go along. And he'd been on track all the way.

Until that night.

It hit him again, hard, the memory of that moment when a tiny little girl had nestled into his hands, looking up at him with dark eyes like her mother's. He figured she probably wasn't seeing him, not really, but it surely seemed as if she were peering into his dark, bruised soul.

He'd been right. This was insane. It made no sense. It was only a baby, one he would likely never see again. So why did he feel as if there were some sort of connection between them, him and that tiny bit of squalling humanity? Just because he'd had the misfortune of being there at her birth? Just because he'd been the first one to touch her, hold her, because he'd been the one to make sure she was breathing and clean and dry and warm?

It made no sense, he repeated to himself.

Now, her mother, that made sense. She was a beautiful woman, a woman any man would take notice of. Even here, where olive-skinned beauties were common, she stood out.

But this puzzled him, too. Because it wasn't simply her looks—she had been swollen with child and under the worst of circumstances when he'd first seen her—but her quiet courage under those circumstances had him thinking about her often. Too often. She was occupying his thoughts unlike any woman ever had.

And he didn't even know her name.

He was so lost in his contemplations that he nearly missed his turn. He yanked the wheel left and headed into the brush along a barely visible track that wound into the back country, where anything could be lost forever.

As he got closer to the selected meeting place, he checked the cubby in the door of the truck where he'd hidden the handgun, a Glock 17, they'd given him after the crash course in using it. But going armed into a meeting with Alcazar would be the height of idiocy, and he was hoping he was past that kind of foolishness. It was secure, and they'd have to literally tear the truck apart to find it, so he felt reasonably sure they wouldn't.

His government-issue cell phone rang. He reached for it automatically, then stopped. That was one advantage to working out here in the vast expanse of empty space; he could always claim he hadn't gotten the call due to lack of signal. He supposed they had ways to verify that, but unless he abused the excuse, he doubted it was worth it to them. And he usually called them back before too much time had passed.

It was a silly, perhaps childish game, but it gave him the

illusion of some kind of control, and right now he would take what little he could get. He didn't want to tell them about what had happened at the ranch.

He wasn't even sure why, if he was afraid they'd chew him out for violating what they called protocol, stepping out of his undercover role and being seen, or if he just wanted to keep it to himself. It almost felt as if telling anyone would violate a promise he hadn't even made, to a courageous woman and a newborn he'd helped bring into the world.

And that made less sense than anything, he thought as he checked the truck's odometer and began scanning for the small building he'd been told to look for.

When he spotted the ramshackle shed, he thought he must be wrong; this wasn't a building, it was a lumber pile in the making. Alcazar wouldn't hang out here. But then, would the man trust him enough to let him know where he really hung out? Ryder knew if he were in Alcazar's position, he would trust no one.

Just as she trusted no one, he thought, the image of that dark-eyed beauty snapping vividly into his mind once more.

Annoyed at himself, he shoved the image away, forcing himself to concentrate. Hadn't it been hammered into him during his weeks of training at that super-secret facility, that lack of focus could be fatal?

So focus, he ordered himself silently.

As he drove up to the tumbledown shack, he spotted a gleam of silver from behind it, the bumper of another car. So it *was* the right place, he thought, unable to imagine any other reason for a car to be all the way out here.

And then, seemingly out of nowhere, the truck was surrounded by armed men. Four of them, automatic pistols at the ready, and all trained on him. His gut knotted, but he kept his hands on the steering wheel in plain sight. The last thing he wanted was to give them an excuse to shoot. And with these guys it wouldn't take much.

The other vehicle was, absurdly, a stretch limo. But then Ryder remembered something he'd heard long ago, before he'd been tossed in prison—that Alcazar liked to conduct his meetings in what he called his "mobile office." This had to be it.

The biggest of the welcoming committee gestured him toward the limo. One of the others opened the passenger side rear door. When he didn't move quickly enough to please the third man, he got a jab with the barrel of the weapon he held.

For a split second, Ryder considered taking the man's head off. Only knowing it would be the last thing he'd ever do stopped him, at least long enough to rein in his temper.

He climbed into the back of the limo.

"Wise choice," said a voice from the far corner.

Ryder didn't pretend not to understand. "Patience is one of my new virtues," he said, but added with a glance back at the man who'd shoved him, "along with a very long memory."

Laughter, rough but tinged with genuine amusement, echoed in the car. Ryder could see Alcazar now, dressed to perfection in a light gray suit and a hat that was a cross between Clay's white Stetson and something a pimp on the streets of Dallas would wear.

"Duane is a bit…energetic, but he's also useful."

"I'm sure. For now." That earned him a jab with the deadly weapon. Ryder merely glanced at it. "I prefer an old-fashioned revolver, myself. It never jams, so you never need to stall, pretending to negotiate with a rattlesnake."

The man being discussed muttered something under his breath, which got him a sharp rebuke from the man in the hat. At further orders, the armed men retreated, shutting the limo's door after them.

"Carbone in Laredo tells me I can trust you."

"He did. It paid off for him."

"So he says."

Ryder said nothing more. He learned never to volunteer more information than was asked for. Besides, he had little else to say on the subject. He wasn't about to let Alcazar know that the man whose word he seemed to value was one of theirs, a government agent going into his third year of undercover work along the border.

The silence stretched out until finally Alcazar said, "You're the silent type, aren't you?"

"I'm not a salesman," Ryder said with a shrug. "Either you trust me or you don't; you have work for me or you don't. You're the boss; you decide."

The laughter came again, and this time it was appreciative. "Would that all of my men had that view."

Ryder shrugged again, this time saying nothing.

"I'm curious, Mr. Grady," Alcazar said.

Ryder lifted a brow, but said nothing. He was used to the name. He'd spent the early years of his life with it, the name of the mother who had never told them who their real father was, the father who had so little interest in them that they'd never laid eyes on him since before Georgie was born. It didn't take a genius to figure out that the name Colton in Texas—or anywhere else these days—would draw more attention than he wanted.

He could just hear Alcazar's reaction if he explained, "Hey, yeah, my bio-dad's brother is *that* Colton, the one who's probably going to be president. But don't worry, I'm still an outlaw...."

"Why would you want to get involved again in the very thing that got you time as a guest of the federal government?" Alcazar asked.

"Because I wasn't involved in it before, and I got hung for it anyway."

He knew the answer was flip, even absurd, but he also knew Alcazar was reputed to have a slightly warped sense of humor. Ryder was gambling on that.

His gamble paid off with the biggest laugh yet. "Might as well be hung for a sheep as a lamb, is that it?"

"Something like that."

"This would be different."

"Different?"

"The package to be transported would be…smaller."

Ryder's breath stopped, his brain screaming that this was it, but he masked his reaction.

"Easier," he said neutrally.

"Not necessarily."

Ryder pretended to consider this, then shrugged. "At least with you I know what I'm getting into."

"Kissing ass, Mr. Grady?"

"No. Just didn't like being a useful idiot."

There was a moment of silence before a rather bemused, "Well, well…"

Ryder said nothing, just waited. That had been close enough, he wasn't about to risk saying anything that might make Alcazar too curious about just who exactly he was.

"I may have something for you. Be ready. Available."

He stopped, as if he expected questions. Ryder asked none. After a moment Alcazar nodded in approval.

"Go. I'll be in touch."

Ryder nodded, took the words as dismissal, and moved toward the door. Then he stopped, glancing back.

"May I punch Mr. Energetic?"

A final laugh. "I would prefer that you didn't."

Ryder shrugged. "You're the boss," he said again.

"Yes," Alcazar said. "I am."

Ryder left it at that. He wasn't about to rock the boat anymore. Not when he apparently had finally broken through; a smaller package could only mean one thing.

A baby.

He was in.

Chapter 6

Ana yawned as she put Maria back to bed. It was only ten o'clock, but she was ready for bed herself. Her little girl seemed to have a voracious appetite, demanding to be fed every two or three hours round the clock. She'd read that this would ease as the baby grew, but for right now it was exhausting.

A light from the hallway glowed under her closed bedroom door. Jewel again? Ana wondered. Did the woman never sleep? She had been so concerned about Ana. After recovering from the shock of finding that the baby had arrived during her absence, Jewel insisted that Ana see a doctor, then rest as much as she could for the next few days. Yet she herself continued her string of sleepless nights.

Now that Ana had her own reason for restless nights and broken sleep, she was even more amazed that Jewel had managed to keep going, suffering seemingly endless insomnia. She did not think Jewel had slept an entire night since she herself had been here, and it only seemed to be getting worse.

And more than once this week when she had been up for a middle-of-the-night feeding with Maria, she had heard Jewel cry out in the darkness. The first time, she had run to her assistance, afraid something had happened. But Jewel had assured her it had only been a bad dream. Ana ached for her new friend, trying to imagine what it must be like for sleep to be so hard to come by, and then, when at last it did, for it to be so haunted by horrible dreams.

She hoped Maria's vocal demands to be fed in the night weren't further disturbing the already-weary Jewel. But the woman never failed to gush over Maria whenever she saw her, and always offered to take her for a while if Ana needed to rest, or do something else. It was such a relief to have someone she truly trusted at hand, yet Ana took care not to overburden the woman who was clearly already carrying a heavy load.

Ana opened her door now, and made her way down the hallway toward the kitchen where the light was. Jewel had been more than kind and generous to her, and she would do whatever she could to help.

She stopped just short of the kitchen doorway when she heard voices. Jewel's and a man's. She leaned forward just enough to see that the visitor was the handsome deputy, Adam Rawlings. And that he was holding Jewel in a comforting embrace.

Ana backed up quickly, not wanting to intrude on what seemed like a tender moment. She had guessed the first time she had seen them together that the deputy was interested in Jewel—it was hard to miss; the man watched her like a hungry cat. But she also knew that Jewel was not interested, not really. She had told Ana that Adam had been very kind, but that she was not ready.

Ana assumed that Jewel's hesitation was because of her old relationship, and had wondered if it ever got any better, if any woman could truly hope to find a man who would not leave or let her down in the end.

A picture popped into her mind, of a tall, dark stranger, with piercing eyes and a dangerous edge. She had sensed the danger about him, although his spine-tingling grin when Maria had let out her first squall had momentarily wiped out all Ana's concerns.

And when the time had come, when her little girl had arrived, he had handled her with exquisite care, with trembling hands and a look of utter awe that had somehow reassured Ana even more.

With an effort that surprised her, she pushed the vivid image out of her mind. She took care with her footsteps as she turned to go. She did not want either Jewel or Deputy Rawlings to know she'd nearly walked in on them.

And then she heard Jewel say three words that stopped her in her tracks.

"...lost my baby."

She whirled back, her heart hammering in her chest. Jewel had lost a baby. Once again, Ana's sympathies went out to the woman. She knew what it was like to lose a child. To have lost both her child and her fiancé at the same time, in a tragic accident, was something Ana could not begin to imagine. Her own loss, of a man not worth having, seemed petty in comparison. Jewel had clearly loved her Andrew, having found him after a long, confusing time in her life.

And the baby...

"So you can see," Jewel told the deputy, who was patting

her gently. The man clearly cared for Jewel, his affection was obvious. "I know what Ana is afraid of. I know what it means to lose a baby."

Adam Rawlings murmured something Ana could not hear, but she was certain they were words of comfort, consolation. For a selfish moment she hoped that he was saying they were close to cracking the smuggling ring, for only then could she breathe easy.

She might be selfish, but she was also thinking of Jewel. When it became clear the topic of the baby-smugglers was not going any further, she retreated to her room and carefully, silently closed the door.

She sat on the edge of her bed, glancing over at the crib now set up just a few feet away. Had she lost a baby so tragically, she was not sure she could bear having another woman's under her roof. Yet Jewel had never given any indication that Ana and Maria were anything less than welcome here at Hopechest. Ana ached anew for her friend.

And marveled anew at her brave spirit.

Perhaps there truly were more good people than bad in the world.

And she could not seem to stop herself from wondering which category her rescuer, and Maria's, fell into.

"I'm still on the ranch," Ryder said into the phone. "I think I'm in, and that there's going to be a move soon, but I don't want to take a chance on missing something else."

"Good thinking."

Ryder's mouth quirked; that was something he hadn't often been accused of in his life. He'd reported in on the approach from Alcazar, which had pleased his handlers, even Furnell, although he hadn't been able to stop himself from giving Ryder a lecture on how critical it was that he not do anything to blow this now.

Ya think? Ryder had muttered silently, but kept the sarcasm to himself.

He ended the call and closed the phone. They'd accepted his explanation of why he was still here easily enough.

Maybe it was even partly true.

He lifted the high-powered binoculars to his eyes, scanning the area around the Hopechest building. It sat in the most distant corner of what had been Bar None land, a piece they'd never been able to use much. Clay had often talked about selling it, although Ryder hadn't paid much attention to such things; he'd sworn early on never to be owned by duty the way his brother was.

And look where that got you, Ryder thought as he turned the binoculars back toward the adobe-and-tile ranch house.

His heart leapt up into his throat, stopping his breath.

There she was.

She had the baby in her arms, wrapped in a pinkish-looking blanket. Very girly, Ryder thought. For a beautiful little girl.

His own thoughts startled him. Again. It was just a baby. One of those squirmy, noisy, red-faced, funny-looking creatures he'd never been comfortable around. The ones who messed, spit up, drooled and woke you at all hours of the night.

Okay, so this was different. This was the only baby he'd ever been this close to. Certainly the only one he'd ever helped bring into the world. It had been an odd feeling, a new one. But he hadn't expected it to last, hadn't expected to feel much more than the lingering curiosity, speculation and mild affection he'd had for the sorrel colt he'd once helped deliver, or Daisy's pups that time.

But this was different.

And he wasn't at all sure what it was.

Maybe it was that he'd never really felt completely connected to another person before. He wasn't capable of that kind of feeling, hadn't even really missed the closeness of family, had instead felt as if he'd escaped when he'd cut all ties with them. He felt the occasional jab of wistfulness for the days when Georgie had tagged after him, but she'd clearly grown up and moved on, changed forever by the birth of her daughter.

And that scary thought brought him jolting back full circle as he watched the woman he'd shared those most intimate of moments with. She cuddled the tiny bundle in her arms. She'd been so incredibly courageous, determined to protect her baby even while doubled over in the agony of labor. She'd fought hard, without the help of drugs, medical equipment, or experienced hands.

She'd had only his hands, and had taken their help only reluctantly.

That was a lucky baby, he thought. And she could do a lot worse than try to grow up like her firebrand of a mother.

He wondered, not for the first time, where the baby's father was. He could understand how the news of a baby would panic a guy, but how the hell could a man walk away from a woman like that?

Maybe he's like you, Ryder thought grimly.

He knew he wasn't capable of being in love. He'd never even been close, wasn't sure he even knew what it meant. He knew love existed, he'd seen it in others, but for himself it was an abstract and romantic notion and he'd dismissed the possibility early on. He'd had his share of women—okay, maybe more than his share—but he'd never once found one he couldn't walk away from without a backward glance.

And he hadn't now, he told himself firmly. Certainly not a woman he'd been with for all of a few hours in the darkness—not that he hadn't done that before, too, but definitely not like this—and whose name he didn't even know.

But sitting here now, looking down at her, seeing her with the baby who'd slipped into his hands, he couldn't deny that he felt...something. A tightness in his chest, a sort of yearning.

He let out a short, sharp bark of laughter at the ridiculous word as it formed in his mind.

Yearning.

Yeah, right. Him, Ryder Grady Colton. Really a yearning sort of guy.

Not that it would matter if it were true. He was a long, long way from getting clear of the mess he'd gotten himself into, and until he finished this job and got that free pass and expunged record, he had no business doing anything but focusing on the job he had to do.

The thought that a baby that wasn't even his could change him forever, the way it had changed his sister, was the most absurd thought of all.

Chapter 7

"You're sure you wouldn't like to come? I'd love for you to meet Tamara."

Ana shook her head and smiled at Jewel. "Perhaps in a few days. I am still very nervous about Maria."

She regretted causing the shadow that flickered in Jewel's eyes. But the woman nodded in understanding.

"Better to be safe," she said. "That baby-stealing ring is still operating, and the fewer people who know about Maria the better, until it's broken up. Some of Tamara's old CSI colleagues are at the ranch now, looking for clues."

Ana was heartened by that news, that the authorities were still working in the area. "That is good."

"I'm worried about Clay, though," Jewel said. "He's taking his brother's death very hard."

Ana frowned. "This is the brother who was in prison?"

Jewel nodded. "He wasn't a bad kid, really, just a little wild. He didn't know what he was getting into."

A bit cynical about criminals claiming innocence, Ana said nothing, not wanting to dispute Jewel's assumption.

"I think the fact that he didn't even claim Clay as next of kin, that he put down he had none on the prison forms, didn't even use their name, really got to Clay. He didn't even find out he was dead until seven months after it happened, when he went to the prison to find out why his letters came back undeliverable."

"I am sorry for his pain," Ana said. That, at least, she could honestly say.

"Tamara told me Clay tried so hard. Not many eighteen-year-olds who would take on the task of raising two younger siblings. But Clay did. And he feels responsible, guilty that he couldn't keep his little brother out of trouble."

"No one," Ana said carefully, "has more power to hurt us than the ones we most love."

Ana felt Jewel's gaze sharpen, and regretted speaking even those vague words. But Jewel kept her word, to ask no questions Ana did not want to answer, and once again Ana silently thanked her.

As she watched Jewel load up the kids for another trek to the Bar None for pony rides, Ana was very happy that her benefactor had found a new friend. And if she found it odd that Tamara and Clay Colton were by all appearances back together again, with the one-time forensics expert happily settled back at the Bar None, she kept the thought to herself. She knew nothing about their relationship.

It was a lesson she'd learned in the hardest of ways, when everyone told her she should turn a blind eye to Alberto's dealings, just as they had told her she had no right to judge her father. They were impressed by her father's polish, his education, the whole, false package. They had called her an idealistic fool to expect any man to turn his back on a lucrative career, just because she did not like some aspect of it.

The illegal aspect of it, she thought. The taking of things they had not earned, from people who had worked hard. The selling of evil, destructive things they called simply "commodities," never caring what the drugs did or the lives they destroyed. The coercion of innocent people to help in their "work," coercion by threat to families, children…

She was not sure which disturbed her more, the actual activities, or the urging of those around her to look the other way. Perhaps she was a naïve, idealistic fool, but she refused to have her baby grow up in a place where such things were accepted.

Alone again, she checked on Maria, who was napping peacefully. She decided she felt up to resuming some of the tasks she had taken on before, in an effort to earn her keep. Jewel had told her not to worry, not to push herself too hard so soon after the birth, but after nearly a week she was restless.

And really, other than feeding and bathing Maria, she had little to do; the children at Hopechest had seemed fascinated by Maria, and the girls especially were always offering to help. Ana suspected they looked upon the baby as an animated doll of some sort, but she still found their wide-eyed interest touching.

At the same time, she looked at these children with a quiet determination that Maria would never end up needing help like this. She would always be there for her little girl, making sure she always knew she was loved. For that was what she saw most in the too-old eyes in the too-young faces around her here. So few of these children had ever been certain they were loved.

"You will always know, *mija,*" she told her sleeping child. "You will always know."

* * *

"You all right, boy?"

Ryder sighed, knowing it must be bad if Boots could tell even over the phone that he was in an uproar.

"Things are just...complicated," he said.

"Life is," Boots agreed. "That's why the Boss gave us brains, to figure it out."

"Yeah, well, I could use a better one just now, then."

"Nothing wrong with your brain, Ryder. How you've used it on occasion, well, that's another story."

The teasing was gentle, and Ryder took no offense. Boots had his best interests at heart, and that was something Ryder had never honestly believed of anyone before in his life. Except maybe his mother, but Mary Lynn Grady had spent most of her too-short life struggling to support her three children sired by, but never acknowledged by, Graham Colton, the profligate brother of the current presidential front-runner.

Ryder had heard some wonder if Joe Colton was fit to be president, with a brother like Graham. Ryder had never been one of them. After all, didn't Clay, straight-arrow, upstanding, good-man-to-the-core Clay, have a brother like him?

What he'd never understood was what his mother had seen in the clearly sleazy, too-slick Graham Colton.

"What are you thinking about, boy?"

Startled, Ryder chided himself for this newly born tendency to get lost in thought.

"My mother," Ryder said, "and how I wish I'd known her before."

"Before?"

Before she got tangled up with my bio-dad, he thought.

"Before she gave up the rodeo," he said. "She must have been something. All fire and sass. But all I ever knew was the woman who got up before dawn every day to work in that diner."

"And you find that less appealing than being a rodeo rider?"

"Well, yeah," Ryder said, barely managing not to add "Of course!"

"Even though she did it for you?"

"You see, that's what I hate about it. Woman gets pregnant, and her life like…ends. She gives up her dreams, like nothing else matters but the kid. Or she dies young, like my mother did. She was only forty-six."

And while that still seemed old to him, he knew that it was far too young to die.

"So why don't you tell me," Boots began, in that tone Ryder had come to know meant some heavy thinking was coming his way, "what it is that's more important than raising kids?"

"I'm not saying it's not important, I know, they turn into adults someday and they'll be in charge, I know all that, but—"

"Did you miss having a father, Ryder?"

"Not mine," he said sourly.

"Agreed. Yours left a lot to be desired. But a father like you might imagine? One who cared about you, was involved in your life, one you could look up to?"

"I guess," Ryder said.

"Do you think things might have gone differently if you'd had one?"

"Maybe."

"Do you think your brother might have been a little more relaxed if there had been a father around to do the things he took upon himself, at far too young an age?"

"Sure."

"And perhaps your sister might have avoided falling for a smooth-talking city boy?"

He'd had enough. "What's the point, Boots?"

He could almost see the leathery old man shrug, could hear in his voice that lopsided smile that meant he was about to drive it home.

"Your biological father thought everything was more important than the kids."

Ryder felt as if he'd been sucker punched. Boots was too damned good at that, led you down the path to exactly where he wanted you to go, then hit you between the eyes.

"Damn it, Boots," he muttered.

There was a moment of silence before the man asked, "What's brought this on, boy? Why are you thinking about all this now?"

He almost spilled it, right then and there. But he couldn't, he knew he couldn't. If he'd tell anyone it would be Boots, but not now, not on a cell phone, not on a phone at all. There was no way in hell he was going to try and explain what had happened the other night over the phone. Hell, how could he explain something he himself didn't understand?

I helped deliver a baby, Boots. For the gutsiest, most beautiful woman I've ever seen. And now I can't get it out of my head. Her…or the baby.

"I don't even *like* babies," he muttered. "They're messy, they throw up on you—"

Boots voice was suddenly sharper. "You haven't done anything stupid, have you boy? Get some girl in trouble?"

"No!"

There had been, admittedly, that girl in New Mexico, when he'd been out of Lone Star for less than two weeks. He'd gone a little crazy, he knew, but it had been a long time. When the sexy little blonde had laughed at him, saying he made love like he'd just gotten out of jail, he'd laughed with her, but he hadn't gone back.

And he'd been, as he always was, careful. No trail of bastards across the country for him.

"It's just this whole…thing I'm working on. It's hard for me to understand."

"Of course it is. You're a decent human being, Ryder."

Ryder laughed. "Now there's something I don't hear much of."

"Take it from a man who was not at one time. I know them when I see them."

Boots didn't often refer to his past. He'd once told Ryder that the man he had once been was dead and buried, and his evil ways with him. To Ryder's amazement he hadn't been bitter at the prospect of spending the rest of his life locked up, despite being a changed man. He didn't even make a true effort at seeking parole, something he'd once explained to a puzzled Ryder.

"Not many believe in jailhouse conversions," he'd said simply. "And I can't blame them. They see it as a criminal's way to try and get out, convince everyone you've found religion so they'll let you go. I won't belittle my faith in that way. And," he'd added, "I have a lot to atone for. Here is as good a place as any to do that."

A lot to atone for…

He remembered how that had hit him, hard. He'd always thought atonement had to be forced on you, like when Clay would order him to apologize to Georgie for teasing her, or that it was something akin to his going to jail, to make up for being stupid enough to get fooled into driving a truck in coyote territory without being sure of what was inside it.

He'd never thought about what it would take to make a

man feel that from inside himself, to feel like he needed to atone for his transgressions, and to proceed to do so in his own way, with no one forcing it on him, no judge ramming it down his throat.

Simply because it was right.

That was the turning point, he realized now. That was the moment when he'd begun to look at Boots not just as a fellow inmate who was older and wiser in the ways of prison life, not just as a man who'd done far worse than Ryder had ever thought of, but as a man who had found something Ryder had never known—a solid, unshakable center, a path to follow and the strength to walk it.

Ryder was no Holy Roller, but when it came right down to it, he didn't think the source of the strength Boots had mattered as much as how he used it. And for some reason he'd chosen to use that strength to help Ryder find his own way.

"You know what the right thing is, Ryder, whatever it is that's eating at you. You just need to let down that guard of yours enough to see the answer."

They'd hit the end of Boots's allotted phone time, and had to say a hasty goodbye. But long after he'd disconnected, Ryder sat thinking.

So what was the right thing? Was Boots right? Was the answer right in front of him—he just couldn't see it?

He shook his head sharply. It was time for him to get back to work. He needed to check the perimeter of the Bar None. There was always a chance of more tunnels that hadn't been found yet. But he wanted to be back at his usual observation post at Hopechest by 2:00 a.m.; he'd seen that somewhere around two or three, the baby usually awakened and her mother got up to feed her.

Tonight was no exception. It was 2:15 a.m. when the light in that front room came on.

Even from a distance, through the high-powered binoculars, the sight of that mysterious, lovely woman with the baby he'd brought into the world at her breast, was the most incredible thing he'd ever seen. It was as if all the pain she'd endured was forgotten, as if the bloody, sloppy mess of the delivery had never happened, all of it wiped away by the miracle she now held in her steady, loving arms.

Had his mother felt like that? She'd been alone, too, thanks to his useless father.

There it was again, that odd, uncharacteristic sense of connection. He'd never felt it before, and now that he couldn't seem to get rid of it, he didn't know what to do about it. He'd always thought being a loner was easier—no strings, no ties, no responsibilities. But the sight of this woman, alone and frightened and yet ready to fight for the child she hadn't even laid eyes on yet, had given him a whole different view of being alone.

And the sight of her now made him feel his own isolation in a way that dug deep.

That famous guard Boots had mentioned seemed useless when it came to this woman.

And to that tiny human she held.

The baby was wrapped in a different blanket this time, something again pink, but with big flowers printed on it. Girly stuff, he thought again, with a smile that surprised him. He didn't know much about that, girly stuff. Georgie had always been a tomboy of sorts, more interested in horses than dolls, and the rodeo schedule always won out over a social calendar. And he'd never been with a woman long enough to really get to know the ins and outs of all that...frilliness.

But the baby's mother didn't seem like the frilly sort. Courageous, definitely. Beautiful, obviously. Tough, absolutely. And he suspected he should throw smart into the mix as well.

And classy.

That was the word that had eluded him until now, when he was watching her tend to her baby with gentle care. Something about her made him picture her in some sleek, designer outfit, turning heads….

As he drove back to the motel in the minutes just after dawn, he thought about that. And he couldn't quite reconcile his image of her with his image of the frightened, desperate illegals that he'd discovered—at the same time as the border patrol agents—in the back of that truck he'd been tricked into driving.

Obviously, one of his assumptions, his images, was wrong.

Maybe both, he thought wryly.

Chapter 8

"...presidential campaign of front-runner Joe Colton will be heading to Texas, where the scandal-plagued candidacy of disgraced Governor Allen Daniels has ground to a halt. Colton and his wife, Meredith, plan a joint visit in a few weeks."

Ryder sipped his coffee in front of the small, motel television. As he watched the video clip of the surging candidate and his wife, he found himself studying them dispassionately. As if they were any other couple in the news, nothing to do with him.

Joe Colton was a tall, lean man in his late sixties. Ryder had heard some time ago that he was an accomplished and lifelong horseman. He'd thought of Clay and Georgie then, and wondered idly if such things were passed on genetically.

Colton's dark hair was peppered with gray, and pure gray at the temples, giving him a distinguished look; any hint of his age was belied by his obvious fitness and his ease of carriage.

As the video played on, Ryder shifted his focus to Meredith Colton, Joe's wife of nearly forty years. She was trim but curvy, and dressed in a classic suit that showed she still had a great pair of legs. Her golden-brown hair was in one of those chin-length cuts that swung as she moved. Her eyes were a warm brown, and sparkled with a kindness that seemed very genuine. She was a classy woman.

Odd, that wasn't a word he often thought of, and yet now he'd done it twice in a day, about two very different women. He frowned. At least, he thought it was today…he had to think to remember if it had been before or after midnight that he'd had the thought about the woman at Hopechest Ranch.

He took another sip of coffee as the report ended with a mention that several of the Colton children, both biological and fostered, would be joining them periodically on the campaign trail.

His cousins, he thought suddenly.

The coffee suddenly tasted bitter, and he dumped it down the motel sink.

Joe Colton and his wife, it seemed, had hearts big enough to take in a multitude of kids not their own. They had even taken in the daughter of Meredith's late sister, who had tried her best to destroy her sister's life.

It was that daughter who was given the chance to run the Hopechest Ranch here in Esperanza. He'd even seen her and had no trouble recognizing her; the woman he'd spotted at the ranch looked just like Meredith Colton.

It occurred to him yet again to wonder how this whole Hopechest Ranch thing had happened. Before he'd gone to prison, the place hadn't even existed. How had it ended up here, on the Bar None of all places? Had Clay somehow joined the Colton fold? Just how much had he been involved in this decision? Was there more to this than merely the sale of some land Ryder knew Clay had been thinking about unloading for a long time? Had Joe and Meredith Colton decided Clay was worthy of inclusion in the illustrious Colton dynasty?

His mouth quirked wryly at the string of questions shooting through his mind. This was getting old fast, this constant wondering and introspection. It occurred to him then that perhaps he was dodging the real question that would likely never be answered. Which was why Graham Colton, so obviously unlike his brother Joe, couldn't even be bothered to acknowledge—let alone care about—children he had actually fathered himself, Ryder thought sourly.

A Colton family portrait flashed on the screen. In it, Joe Colton was seen wearing his trademark dazzling smile. Every time he saw a picture of that smile, Ryder had felt an odd sensation, not quite uneasiness, but a sort of twitchiness it had taken him a long time to figure out. When he had—when he happened to have seen a photo of the then senator shortly before having his own photo taken for his driver's license—it had been a jolt he would never forget.

Because Joe Colton's smile, that look that charmed millions, was a dead ringer for his own.

Talk about genetics.

"Get over yourself!" Ryder snapped aloud now.

He'd had about enough of this unaccustomed pondering of the mysteries of life that he'd never bothered himself about before.

"Leave the philosophizing to Boots," he ordered, then nearly groaned as he realized he'd added talking aloud to himself to his list of new and annoying habits.

He turned off the television, starting to wish he'd never turned it on. Knowing he was connected, however tenuously, to the family that seemed to head every newscast and headline every newspaper was too unsettlingly strange for his taste.

Clay, now, he could see that. He'd fit right into that family, with his straight-arrow attitude and oversized sense of responsibility.

"More power to you, bro," he said, meaning it. For his part, he knew the best thing he could do was what he'd done—sever all ties and leave Clay in peace. He was no doubt relieved not to have the burden of worrying about his troublesome little brother.

He glanced at his watch. It was nearly twilight when he could head out for his nightly surveillance. Anticipation kicked through him at the thought of seeing her again, even at a distance. Over the past several nights he'd given up trying to fight the feeling; now he just settled for hoping it would eventually wear off.

In the meantime, he kept an eye on Hopechest Ranch and its environs for his job, and an eye on a young mother and her baby for himself.

His cell phone rang. Not the silly, chirping ring he'd programmed in for his calls from his handlers, but the sharp jangle he'd set for one caller only.

Alcazar.

He went still. This call could possibly be the beginning of the end; if he was really in, it would be a job. And if so, he was on the verge of blowing this ring wide open.

And then he'd be done here, and he didn't know whether to wish for that or not.

On the third ring, he flipped open the phone, making certain his voice was casual, unconcerned as he answered with the name he'd given them, borrowed from his mother and his legendary grandfather. He'd never known "Rattle-snake" Grady, which he'd always regretted; he'd sounded, in the stories his mother had told, like the one relative he would really have liked to have known. How could you not admire a man who could stick eight seconds on the back of a rattler-spooked bull, then kill the snake, and who wore its skin like a talisman in every rodeo he went to until the day he died?

"I have a job for you," the voice on the other end of the phone said without preamble.

Ryder's pulse jumped, but he kept his voice even. "Yeah?"

"Tonight."

"Short notice."

"Is that a problem?"

"Not for me," he said, as if it meant less than nothing to him. "Not if it's worth my while."

Alcazar quoted a figure then, a dollar amount that took Ryder aback for a moment. He'd guessed this business was profitable, but that much, just for a night's work?

"In that case," Ryder said, "you get the platinum service."

To his satisfaction, Alcazar laughed. He wanted to stay on the right side of this man. He didn't think he was the ringleader—he wasn't smart enough—but he was the best lead Ryder had. He had his suspicions about who was really running things, a man who had access and opportunity, but Ryder hadn't pointed him out to his handlers yet. His new bosses had a nasty habit of making moves they didn't tell him about until after the fact. He supposed it was one of the downsides of being a coerced agent rather than a volunteer good guy. Which made no sense to him. He himself would trust somebody who had everything to lose more than the innate desire for law and order some people had.

Maybe because he'd never seemed to develop that desire

himself, he thought wryly as he listened to Alcazar's detailed instructions on where to be in three hours.

When the call had ended, he wondered whether he should let his handlers know it was a go. If he did, they might move into the area and screw up everything. If he didn't, they might just yank him out and toss him back in that prison cell—not a prospect he wanted to deal with. If he had to go back and serve the rest of his interrupted sentence, that would be bad enough. But he had the suspicion that if he blew this, the powers that be would conveniently forget where the key was, and he'd be lost forever in the prison system.

He compromised and, while driving to the rendezvous point set up in the earlier call, made the official report and told them most of it.

"I don't know what the job is. Not for sure." That was true. "I have to meet with them again, then maybe I'll find out."

"Report in as soon as you know," Furnell ordered.

"Yeah."

Feeling like a puppet on too short a string, he snapped the phone shut sharply. And once again pondered the possibility of just running, leaving all this behind and taking off. He always felt like this after talking to Furnell.

But he didn't want to spend the rest of his life looking over his shoulder, slipping down into a pit of paranoia until he saw the feds behind every tree.

Running wasn't really an option; he was just flailing around looking for an escape that wasn't there. As Boots told him, he should be glad for this chance to make things right, a chance few got. If he pulled this off he'd be free and clear, his record clean and no need to check that damn little box on any form asking if he'd ever been convicted of a felony.

He made the turn as instructed and continued to drive, now on a rough, dirt, two-rut track, the truck's headlights pushing back the utter darkness out here in the remote, unlit ranch country. With the windows rolled down in the night heat of August, the scent of warmed mesquite blew through the truck's cab.

It was a familiar scent to him, although he denied feeling any kind of nostalgia for it; it was just nice to be out, and not locked up where this kind of isolation and peace and quiet was impossible. He'd never thought of himself as a loner, not really, but he'd found that the simple privilege of privacy was one of the things he'd missed most in prison.

This was a different location than the last meeting, in the opposite direction and many miles farther off the main road. It was also very close to the western border of the Bar None, near Hopechest. He hoped the world he'd left behind and the world he'd landed in now weren't going to collide before this was all over.

What he would do then, when it was over, he didn't know.

The first thing that popped into his head was an image of a beautiful, olive-skinned woman and a tiny baby. She—well, both she's—had gotten under his skin like no one ever had, and he didn't like the feeling.

Once he got out of this, got away from here, he was sure he could regain his usual nonchalance about such things. It was the forced proximity as much as anything else that had kept them in the forefront of his mind—he was sure of that. Once he took off, it would all fade away. He'd be glad to be gone, he told himself. There were too many memories here anyway.

Somehow seeing the Bar None every day, seeing life going on, knowing his little sister had gotten married, seeing his brother apparently cozying up once more with his ex-wife, just pounded home how little he belonged here. His absence obviously hadn't even left a ripple, so there was no point in sticking around.

This kind of life wasn't for him, anyway. He wasn't the kind to settle down to life in a little burg like Esperanza, getting married and raising a bunch of rug rats...

Even as the thought flitted through his mind, the images played back in his head again—of the tiny little girl, who moments before had been merely an abstract concept, but had suddenly become the most real thing he'd ever seen. And his had been the first human touch she'd known....

He shook his head, angry at himself now. He needed to be focusing on what was about to happen, not some silly, rose-colored memory probably half-imagined by now anyway.

Boots would laugh if he could see him now.

As soon as the words ran through his mind, he knew they weren't true. If Boots could see him now, and know what he was thinking, how he was thinking, Ryder knew exactly what the old man would do.

He'd sit there as he always did, smiling that annoying smile that said he saw more than you'd ever wanted him to, and nodding wisely as if he'd expected this all along.

"You set me up for this, damn it," he muttered in the darkness of the truck's cab.

And then he nearly groaned anew at the ridiculousness of trying to blame an old man locked up miles away for his own screwed-up thoughts. He'd thought he'd gotten past that old dodge, blaming others for the results of his own poor decisions. Lord knew, Boots had spent enough time hammering the lesson into his head.

Telling himself he'd do better to remember the lessons pounded into him at that secret training facility, he reached down with his left hand and pulled the Glock out of the hidden compartment. He shifted in the truck seat and shoved the weapon into his belt at the small of his back.

Then he settled in and drove on through the night.

Chapter 9

Ana thought the evening would never end. She had only reluctantly agreed to accompany Jewel and the younger children on this trip into town. Only Jewel's firm and caring insistence made Ana acquiesce.

She had been nervous about being seen out in public, with her uncertain status until the long, laborious process of obtaining her legal papers was completed. But Jewel was nothing if not determined and kept at her to leave the ranch. And Ana suspected she had put more than a little of her vast knowledge of human psychology to work in the process as well.

Most of all, of course, Ana had been nervous about leaving Maria. Jewel guessed this easily. Things had been very, very quiet lately, she had said, with a knowing look that told Ana exactly what she meant; there had been no further smuggling activity. Ana supposed Deputy Rawlings had told Jewel this, so it must be true.

And while she knew Nicole, the older girl who had volunteered to watch the baby, was reliable, no one could look out for her child the way she herself could.

In the end, Jewel had been persuasive. She owed so much to this generous woman with such tragedy in her past, it was impossible to say no to her.

And it was nice to get out. A little, at least. Despite her nervousness, she enjoyed meeting Becky French, the short, plump woman who ran Miss Sue's. She was a lifelong resident of Esperanza, and knew everyone and everything that happened in the little town.

"We're like that Bogart movie," the woman said, smiling widely, her blue eyes sparkling, "sooner or later, everyone comes to Sue's."

When a little—very little—bit of coaxing from Jewel got the woman to bring out the latest photographs of her grandchildren, Ana found herself looking on with interest. None of them were as beautiful as Maria. Ana laughed at herself; she had become a thoroughly blind, doting mother already.

Cautious, she did not mention Maria despite the urge to share in the joy of new babies. And she was grateful when Jewel didn't mention her either.

I know what Ana is afraid of. I know what it means to lose a baby....

Jewel's tragedy stabbed through to Ana's tender heart. It was nothing short of a miracle that this generous, loving woman could even bear to look at photographs of other women's babies, let alone take one into her home.

Ana felt a sudden, fierce need to go, to be with her baby. She was sure if she made a fuss, Jewel would cut short the outing and take her back to the ranch. But the children were so happy, these youngsters who had had so little happiness in their lives until now, and Ana couldn't bring herself to do it.

I simply should not have come, she told herself. *And I will not again. I will never allow myself to be separated from my baby again. It's far too hard.*

She stirred her melting ice cream into a thick chocolate soup, and waited.

This time the meeting place was a deep gully that would be a ripe pathway for flash floods after a storm. Ryder could see the advantage. You could hide a set of double trailers in there and no one would be able to see them except from an aircraft.

They'd told him to look for a half boulder marked with paint and park there. He soon spotted the bright red slash that gleamed like blood in his headlights. The sides of the gully were less steep here, but steep enough so that his four-wheel-drive truck started to slide a bit. He stopped it on the left side of the boulder as instructed, and then spotted a dark-colored open Jeep down in the bottom of the gully. The motor was still running, the headlights on and aimed his way, as if they wanted to hide in the darkness behind the lights.

Or ruin your night vision, Ryder thought.

On that thought he flicked on his high beams; two could play that game. The added, brighter light showed him two figures standing near the Jeep, and a third one sitting in the driver's seat—planning a quick getaway, perhaps?

He heard one of them swear, then yell at him to kill the lights. He smothered a grin as he hit the control.

"Sorry," he called out. "Didn't want to hit anything. It's dark out here in the boonies."

Just like the rats prefer, he added silently as one of the men called him a name in Spanish that Ryder was sure would have offended his mother, if she were still alive. Ryder smothered a grin as he scrambled down the side of the gully with as much grace as he could manage. The other section of the paint-marked boulder, an even bigger chunk, lay at the bottom.

"Stop right there. Just because the boss trusts you doesn't mean I do," the voice said, confirming Ryder's guess about his identity.

Mr. Energetic. Great.

"Let's get this done, we're wasting time," Ryder said. He wondered if they were going to send him somewhere to pick up a baby. Wondered how the hell they arranged it. Wondered where they found people to help.

Wondered how they slept at night.

Idiot. If they were the kind who'd let that bother them, they wouldn't be doing it in the first place, he told himself.

"Let's go," Mr. Energetic said, swinging a large duffel bag out of the back seat of the Jeep.

"*Let's* go?" Rider asked.

Mr. Energetic laughed, that same harsh sound. "You think the boss is stupid? I'll be coming with you."

"I work alone."

"Then you don't work with us. Which is fine with me, pretty boy."

Ryder had to make a quick decision and he could only see one possibility. He shrugged. "Your funeral," he said, earning a sharp look from Mr. E.

At the man's order he climbed back up the way he'd come down into the gully, not caring for having to turn his back on Mr. E, but hoping clambering up the slope would keep him occupied.

Once they were next to his truck, the man spoke again. "Drive back the way you came. We'll be called with directions on where to take the package," he finished, indicating the bag.

The first thing Ryder thought was that even Mr. E didn't know where they were going yet. The second was that he'd been completely wrong.

Ryder's hopes collapsed as he stared at the zippered bag. He'd obviously misjudged. And despite Mr. E's claim that the boss trusted him, obviously he didn't trust him enough to let him in on the baby smuggling. So what were they having him carry? Was the thing stuffed with coke? Meth? Worse?

He hesitated; this could be a hornet's nest for him. His handlers had let a lot of petty stuff go in the interest of furthering the investigation, but a duffel full of drugs? But he didn't see any way out, and took the handles. The way Mr. E was holding it made the bag seem light to him, as he pictured kilos of white powder or some such jammed into every corner. And he could see now that it wasn't packed as full as he would have expected.

"It's drugged. Should be quiet."

It took a moment, given his thoughts about the contents of the bag, for the odd statement to register.

"What?"

"They give it some kind of cold meds, to keep it asleep." Mr. Energetic gave a harsh laugh. "Don't want the thing crying at the wrong time, now do we?"

Ryder went cold. He wasn't sure what made him queasier, the thought that he'd been wrong, that this really was the break he'd been waiting for, or that they'd apparently stuffed a baby into this bag like so much dirty laundry.

It. The thing.

The words, his own words, echoed in his head, and made him feel slightly ill. He'd talked the same way, with the same lack of concern.

He reached for the zipper on the top of the bag.

"What the hell are you doing?"

"I went to prison for not making sure what I was transporting," Ryder answered. "Not stupid enough to do it again."

The reminder of his prison time seemed to mollify even Mr. E, who let his protest subside as Ryder tugged the zipper halfway open. He peered inside as best he could in the faint light this far from the Jeep's headlights.

His heart slammed in his chest, and his breath stopped in his throat when he saw a wad of cloth wrapped around a tiny bundle.

A blanket.

A familiar blanket.

Pink. With darker pink flowers.

In disbelief he tilted the bag, looked at the tiny face, at the gorgeous skin, the dark hair just like her mother's.

It wasn't just a baby. It was *the* baby. The baby he had brought into the world.

Ryder silently swore the same heartfelt curse the smuggler had. An image of this child's mother flashed through his mind. Of her walking the floor in the middle of the night, nestling this tiny girl to her breast. He remembered, for an instant, the moments when he'd wondered if she was here to simply have this baby and hand it over to the smugglers for a price.

Call him a fool, naive, or any of the other things he was half-sure he was right now, but he didn't believe it. Couldn't believe it.

She wouldn't.

She would not do that.

Which left only one option. Kidnapping.

Which left him only one option.

Chapter 10

Ryder knew the moment he made the move that it was a mistake.

A big mistake.

If he'd thought first—not his greatest strength—he would just played along and taken down Mr. E when they were alone out in the brush somewhere. He could have done it easily.

And probably would have enjoyed it.

But what capacity he had for thinking first seemed to have vanished at the first sight of the baby. Or rather, this baby. Her presence enraged him; the thought of her in the hands of these slime balls for any length of time was damn near unbearable.

So at the first sight of her, he'd promptly forgotten the crash training course the feds had put him through. He did what had gotten him into trouble so often before—went with his gut reaction. He grabbed for the duffel bag.

Forgetting the little problem of four-to-one odds.

He had completely, thoroughly, lost his mind.

With a shout, Mr. E dropped the bag and lunged at him. Ryder spun, took him down with a kick that should have shattered his knee and an elbow to the solar plexus. It gave him time to back up and go for the Glock at his back. Mr. E was writhing on the ground, swearing and staring at Ryder in shock.

Ryder heard the shouts, the sound of the Jeep roaring up the slope like an angry cougar.

Oh, yeah. The other guys, Ryder thought stupidly. Three of them.

He grabbed the duffel bag and backed toward the truck, the Glock trained on Mr. E. The Jeep crested the bank in a spray of dirt, and the three men leapt out.

"Don't shoot him," Mr. E yelled at them. "His ass is mine."

They were running at him, all three of them, guns at the ready. Mac 10s, he guessed from the shape. He held onto his own weapon, the only equalizer he had. He wasn't sure who to train it on. Mr. E didn't seem like the type to inspire enough loyalty to get the other two to put down their guns. Not when they'd have to explain to Alcazar later.

It looked like a standoff.

But he had the baby, and that made him the winner.

I'll get you back to your mother, little one, he promised the baby silently.

"What the...?" one of the armed men asked.

"I knew the boss shouldn't have trusted pretty boy here," Mr. E said, getting to his feet slowly.

Damn, Ryder thought. Guess I didn't break his knee after all.

Then again, when he tried to take a step, the man groaned loudly, and that leg nearly buckled. But he reached under his jacket and took out a matching automatic pistol. And now Ryder was looking at four weapons that could pump him so full of metal he'd probably reflect the Texas sun when they finally found him out here.

If they ever did.

"What the hell do you want with a baby?" the man who'd been behind the wheel asked, sounding more bewildered than anything. "No one's going to deal with you, not with Alcazar running this show."

"Shut up," Mr. E said, and Ryder was pleased to see sweat beading up on his face.

"But he's not a cop, we know that, what the—"

"Just shut up, Denny," one of the other men said, and Ryder got the feeling Denny was the driver because they didn't much trust him to react quickly enough to do anything else.

"Back off," Ryder said, gesturing at them with the Glock.

"Pretty boy can't count," the one who hadn't yet spoken said. "Four of us, one of you, jerk wad."

"Gives me four targets," Ryder said, feigning a cool he was far from feeling. The too-slight weight of the duffel felt like the weight of the world to him in that moment. "I'm not even going to tell you which one I'll shoot first."

"He had to know it was a baby, that's why we're here, so why was he so surprised?" Denny asked.

"Shut *up!*" one of the others said in exasperation.

"He was down for the deal, until he looked at the baby. I think—" that earned the beleaguered driver a chorus of derisive hoots, but he kept on doggedly "—he *knows* that baby."

The hoots of laughter continued. Obviously they weren't terribly worried about him, or his promise to shoot one of them. Not that he could blame them, not at these odds.

The laughter faded into jabs about Denny's thinking abilities, but Ryder's heart sank when he saw that Mr. E, instead of joining the chorus, was looking at him, brows furrowed.

"Shut up," Mr. E said, but this time it was directed at his men.

Ryder suddenly didn't like the taste of this at all.

"Put down that bag," Mr. E said, and there was a world of menace in his tone now.

"Guess that makes you my first target," Ryder said.

"Never mind your first target," Mr. E said. "Here's mine."

And the hand that held his weapon shifted, lowered.

Ryder's stomach clenched, sending a wave of nausea through him.

He was aiming at the baby.

"You won't shoot." It took Ryder a moment to get the words out past the knot in his throat, to pretend a casual callousness he was far from feeling. "Your boss won't like it if you kill his investment."

He hated even talking about the baby that way, but he had to in order to get through this.

Assuming he got through it at all.

"It won't be my problem," Mr. E said easily. "The story will be that *you* killed it."

Ryder's gut clenched anew.

"Put the bag down."

Ryder stared at the man. It was like looking into the cold, reptilian eyes of a venomous Gila monster. And Ryder knew in that moment, without a doubt, that the man would do exactly as he said. He would murder a helpless baby without a second thought.

Ryder set down the bag.

Mr. E gestured at him with his weapon. "Now the gun."

Ryder hesitated; once he gave up the gun, he was toast.

And the baby would vanish, likely never to be found. But if he tried to shoot his way out of here, the baby could end up dead anyway.

Mr. E shifted his aim, once more pointing the weapon at the duffel bag.

"Fifteen bullets per second," Mr. E said, with an evil glee that made Ryder feel deathly cold.

He knew what would happen to him. He felt that at least the baby would survive, in fact would probably have a good life somewhere, with parents willing to pay any amount for a healthy child.

Her mother, he thought, an image of the woman whose name he would now likely never know forming in his mind. The memory of her nerve, her steely determination, had haunted him for days now.

If it were she standing here, what would she do?

She would do whatever it took to protect her baby.

He knew that as surely as he knew his life was counting down right here. She would give up anything, sacrifice anything, to ensure her baby's safety.

He dropped his Glock into the dirt.

When two of them grabbed his arms, he thought they were going to cart him back to Alcazar to decide what to do with him. He even had an instant to plot his escape, but the baby complicated things. He couldn't, wouldn't risk her getting hurt.

And then Mr. E moved, suddenly, putting his full weight behind a pile driver punch.

Pain exploded in Ryder's gut. A starburst of light seemed to blind him for a moment. He thought his lungs must have collapsed under the force and he couldn't draw breath. A second blow made his head spin. A third glanced off his ribs, but set up a whole new kind of pain.

He jerked against his captors but they only tightened their grip, yanking his arms back until his shoulders screamed a protest. Mr. E laughed. The sound matched the look in his eyes when he'd aimed his weapon at the duffel bag.

The first blow to his head made Ryder dizzy. The next snapped his head so hard to one side he thought he felt something rip. The next set up a ringing in his ears that he thought might never go away.

Through the pain, as Mr. E laughed harder and put more power into each blow, Ryder began to realize this wasn't just punishment for stepping out of line.

This was an execution.

Oddly, the idea of dying didn't particularly terrify him. But then if he died no one would know what had happened to that baby.

He had to stay alive. He was the only one who'd gotten this far. If someone came in and had to start over, the baby would be long gone, lost forever to her mother. And her mother would never get over it. He knew that in some bone-deep way.

After Mr. E's next punishing strike, he let himself go limp. His suddenly dead weight broke their hold as he started to sag to the ground. He had to hope neither of them noticed he was keeping his feet under him.

"Our turn now?" the man on his right arm asked hopefully.

"All yours," Mr. E said. "Leave something for the vultures to feed on."

The man who had spoken laughed, and let go of Ryder's arm to step in front and add his own fists to the mix. In that instant Ryder made his move. Ignoring the excruciating pain that wracked him, he yanked his left arm free. For an instant he thought his legs weren't going to cooperate. Then he got them working.

He ran.

He heard the shouted curses. Knew he had only seconds, if that. Heard the first shot. Then a spray of automatic fire. He let out a yell of pain. Stumbled backwards to the crumbling edge of the gully. Flailed wildly. Went over the edge.

In the instant when he hit the split boulder at the bottom of the ravine, heard an ominous snap in his chest and felt a sharp stab of pain, he thought he just might have finished the job for them.

Chapter 11

Ana nearly cried when the kids decided they wanted to stop at the mini-mart, the only business still open this late. It was not that she begrudged them their candy bars, but she wanted to get back to her baby. The stress of separation was about to make her scream out loud.

Since Jewel would allow them only one candy bar each—which, she told them sternly, they would have to save until tomorrow after the ice cream tonight—they talked about getting what they all liked and dividing up the goods among them all. And when two of them discovered a tiny souvenir T-shirt that said, "I found hope in Esperanza," a play on the meaning of the town's name, Ana felt ashamed of herself for wanting to cut their outing short.

"Absolutely," Jewel said with a smile as she held up the little pink shirt. "Maria needs this. It is her color, after all."

Ana touched Jewel's arm, and the woman looked at her. "Your kindness," Ana said softly, "and your courage humble me."

"If you want to talk about courage," Jewel retorted in an equally soft tone, "let's talk about yours."

Ana felt her cheeks warm. Jewel patted her arm in turn. "Let's get you home to your little girl. You've been very good about staying away so long, so these short people here could have some fun."

The kids reacted with groans at the short people joke, but Ana sensed they were not really upset; Jewel and Hopechest Ranch had given these children a sense of belonging, of being valued, that had been sadly lacking in their lives. They were blossoming under the tender care, whether it was on an outing like this, working feverishly at some craft, or playing with the multitude of toys scattered around the ranch house.

Jewel then turned to pay the cashier. When she had the bag in her hands, she explained that she would be holding onto the loot until tomorrow, earning her a chorus of groans. Jewel was not only kind and brave, she was very smart about children, Ana thought. And Ana admired the way she was instilling confidence in all her charges, and responsibility in the older ones, like Nicole.

Ana wondered if perhaps her kindness might extend to teaching Ana what she knew; she needed all the help she could get for the days to come when she would have to raise Maria properly, teach her what was right and wrong, what was important in life.

She herself, so far, could only serve as a bad example, she feared. But that was over now, behind her, and she would never make mistakes like that again.

She would never trust so easily again.

* * *

He wasn't going to make it.

With every step, he knew it. Every time he fell, he knew he couldn't get up again. Every inch he gained, even when he was reduced to crawling through the brush, he knew was the last he could manage.

Yet he kept going.

He thought he passed out a few times, at least he seemed to remember waking up with his face in the dirt, with various insects scurrying over him, in anticipation of his certain death, or perhaps just drawn by the blood. Sometimes the thought of them feeding on him drove him a few precious yards farther. Sometimes he hurt so much he didn't even care.

He told himself that if they hadn't taken his truck and he'd tried to drive, he would have crashed it by now. It didn't make his progress any less torturous. He didn't know how long he'd been crawling. Didn't know how far he'd come. Wasn't even sure he was going in the right direction. He had to hope that his memories of the Bar None were guiding him properly. His conscience jabbed him anew. He had to tell her. Even if he died with his next breath, he had to tell her. She would do what had to be done to save her baby, he knew it. He hated that he'd blown it so badly, that it would be left to her, but it was down to that.

He had to get to her.

He kept on, for what seemed like an endless nightmare trek. Still he was startled when, the next time he forced himself to his feet, he saw the dark shape of Hopechest Ranch looming up in the darkness, just a few yards away. For a moment he thought he was imagining it, that some burst of wishful thinking had his mind seeing things that weren't there in the darkness.

But from the fixture on the front porch, there was a gleam of light near the room where he'd found the beautiful, gutsy woman about to deliver the prettiest little girl he'd ever seen.

He blinked, his dazed mind telling him, belatedly, that it was okay to blink now. It had been the hardest thing he'd ever done, not to blink when Mr. E and his men had shone a bright flashlight down on him at the bottom of the gully. He'd forced himself to keep his eyes open, trying to approximate the blank stare of dead eyes, praying that they wouldn't come down the slope, that his eyes and the twisted, awkward position of his body bent painfully back against the boulder would convince them he was already dead or close enough to it.

He hadn't been sure they weren't right, had been almost afraid to try to move when they'd laughed and gone, afraid that he wouldn't be able to.

But he had. And somehow, he'd gotten here. The sight galvanized him, and he got his feet under him and staggered forward. He was going to get it done, the one thing that had driven him. He had to last long enough to tell her what he knew. It seemed an unfair burden to drop on a woman still recovering from childbirth, but the memory of her quiet courage that night, the steely determination he'd seen in her dark eyes, was the prod that had kept him going; she would do what had to be done, he told himself with every pain-wracked step.

He collapsed in a heap in the shadows beneath her bedroom window.

With a smile, Ana accepted the hugs of the children and the gift they had picked out for Maria. As Jewel led them off to bed, Ana walked down to the family room where a light was on. Nicole was on the couch, fast asleep, the controller for the video game still in one hand. Ana frowned; she had not realized this was what the girl would be doing. She had had an image in her mind of Nicole playing with Maria, as she often did during the day, the girl smiling as her baby cooed. It was the only thing that had enabled her to leave at all.

But perhaps she had only begun to play the game after she put Maria to bed, Ana thought, not wanting to jump to harsh conclusions. She gently took the controller, studied the unfamiliar buttons for a moment until she found the way to turn it off. Then she shut off the television.

Rather than wake Nicole, she took a throw from the back of an adjacent chair and spread it over the sleeping girl. She was good-hearted, surely she would have taken good care of Maria. And she had spoken often of taking care of her little sisters before their parents had tragically been killed.

Still, Ana had to check on her baby right now.

She turned and walked back toward the front of the house. All was quiet there now. She could hear Jewel speaking softly to the young ones, who had apparently followed her instructions in record time, no doubt to make sure they got their selected treats tomorrow. The house went silent so quickly Ana was amazed.

She heard Jewel's footsteps as she went toward her own rooms on the other side of the house. Hoping Jewel would get some real sleep tonight, Ana headed down the hall and stepped into her own room, leaving the light off so as not to wake Maria. She tried hard to keep the baby quiet at night, for Jewel's sake.

She started across the room toward the crib. Her anxiety had lessened now that she was back and all was apparently well. But she still wanted to see her baby. She walked carefully; her rubber-soled sandals tended to squeak on the tile floor, and she didn't want—

The quiet groan from just outside stopped her in her tracks. She barely stifled a scream. Only the realization that whatever it was sounded like it was in great pain allowed her to keep from shrieking the roof down.

The fact that she could not be sure what it was she had heard calmed her instinctive fright a little. The sound had been so muffled, so muted it could have been anything, any kind of animal. That it had come from outside her window was unsettling, but not necessarily terrifying. She thought of calling for help, but the only other adult in the house was Jewel. She couldn't bear to disturb her when she was getting so little sleep anyway, not without knowing what was wrong.

She tiptoed toward the window, keeping carefully to the shadows, thankful she had not turned on the light to betray her presence. The big, comfortable rocking chair, a gift from Jewel, was in front of the window. She stepped around it, thinking that if anything—or anyone—tried to break the window and come in, getting tangled up in that moving chair would give her enough time to grab Maria and make an escape.

Ready to run in an instant, Ana peered out the window.

And nearly screamed again. Instead she sucked in a breath of pure shock, the sound she made tiny and strangled.

There was a man lying on the ground outside her window.

She turned, starting to back away. She would grab Maria and go to Jewel. They would call for help, maybe Deputy Rawlings and—

The man moved. She leapt back, out of any possible line of sight. He groaned again, and there was no mistaking the pain in the sound. And then something registered in her mind, something that made her frown.

His movement had revealed his face. His features were oddly dappled in the light of an ebbing moon, but they registered.

Instead of running, she leaned forward and took a second peek.

It was her white knight, her rescuer, the tall, dark and handsome cliché who had appeared as if magically out of the night and disappeared the same way.

And suddenly everything changed. She still did not trust him, but he had helped her when there was no one else to do it. He had helped bring Maria into the world, had been the first touch her baby had known, and then when she had asked him to, he had gone back the way he had come, no questions asked. That had to be worth something, if not everything.

She had certainly not been able to put him out of her mind as she had hoped. Images of him had interrupted her days and haunted her nights. She had been filled with a strange sense of longing that, no matter how she tried, she could not seem to talk herself out of with any amount of common sense.

She had wished more than once that he could have known who she really was, that she was not just looking for a handout, that she wanted to do things right, was trying to do it the legal way, that she was intelligent, educated, and had skills she could and was willing to put to good use in exchange for a safe life for her and her little girl.

She had never imagined it could matter to her so much what a total stranger thought of her. But it did.

She had tried to tell herself that it was because he had shared that most intimate of times with her, or that it was because he had been like a white knight in a fairy tale, appearing in the nick of time and then vanishing. But part of her new life was a determination to face honestly the realities of the people around her; seeing what was not there, or not seeing what was, had propelled her into this situation to begin with.

And she had realized, during one 2:00 a.m. feeding in that chair, staring out into the moonlit night as Maria suckled, that this new resolution should include being honest with herself as well. That had been the moment when she had admitted that her feelings about her unknown rescuer were much more complicated than simply gratitude for his mysterious and timely help.

And now, here he was, obviously hurt and needing her help in turn. Her need for fairness, her faith in balance and, in an old-fashioned way, her sense of honor demanded she provide it.

She should still wake Jewel, she thought as she hurried around to the front door; opening the garage would make enough noise it might draw someone curious, something she did not want until she had the chance to assess the situation. After all, here was this strange man, on the grounds of her precious Hopechest Ranch. Although Ana did not think he was a threat, that was not really her decision to make.

But first, she must see how badly he was hurt. If he needed medical attention, that would make the decision for her.

Moments later she was crouching beside him, pushing the branches of the privet bush under her window aside to reach him.

The moment she touched him he groaned again, and jerked slightly. His eyes opened, but looked oddly unfocused. Then they sharpened, and she saw that he recognized her.

He smiled.

Ana's breath caught. Never in her life had a man smiled at her like that, in a way that made her heart leap in her chest. That this man would do so now, when he was so obviously in pain, stirred a feeling buried so deep inside her she could not name it, not now. There was no time anyway, things needed to be done, and as he had been for her, she was the only one here to do them.

She leaned in closer, and smothered a gasp of shock when she realized that the discolorations on his face that she had thought were an effect of the moonlight coming through the leaves were instead patches of blood and swollen, reddened flesh. He looked as if he had been beaten, and badly.

Very badly.

"No, no," she whispered when he moved as if he were trying to get up. "You are hurt, you must stay still until we know how badly."

"Walked…forever," he said. "Can't be…that bad."

At least he could speak, she thought. A moment later she wished he could not.

"The baby…your baby."

Ana went still. "What about my baby?"

"Tried…get her away from them."

The sense of what he was saying stabbed through her. "My baby is here. In her crib."

"Saw her…pink flowers."

The blanket, Ana realized. Maria's blanket, that's what he was talking about.

Terror gripped her. Without another thought she leapt to her feet and raced back into the house. This time she hit the light switch the moment she ran into her room, thinking she would never be more grateful to hear Maria cry.

Seconds later she was standing beside her baby's crib, her hands clenched around the rail until every knuckle was white.

Maria was gone.

Chapter 12

Ryder saw the scream forming in her throat.

"Don't," he said.

He'd been able to get up and follow her inside, feeling not quite so horrible after his unintentional rest outside her window. For a brief moment, he'd even allowed himself to hope he'd been wrong, that it hadn't been her baby. How would he know, after all? Barring obvious differences, one baby looked pretty much like another to him.

But he'd known. In his gut he'd known, with a certainty that stunned him almost as much as Mr. E's first punch had.

She whirled then, her dark eyes wide and full of panic. And accusation. She flew at him, her fists up. He held up his hands to ward her off; she might be more than half a foot shorter than he, but he knew her strength, and, coupled with her emotional state, she could do some real damage.

Especially when he was wobbly on his feet already.

"You took her!" the frantic woman spat out, but she stopped in front of him without striking a blow. Lucky for him, he thought. "You are one of them, those despicable men who traffic in innocent babies."

"I'm not. I'm trying—" he had to stop to take in a breath that hurt his ribs "—to stop them. I've been working on cracking the ring."

She didn't look much less suspicious. "I am going to call the sheriff."

Ryder swore inwardly. He was so close, and if she called the sheriff now, it would all be over. He'd be back in the slammer and Maria would be lost forever somewhere up the evil railroad these slimeballs had built.

"We'll lose her," he said, desperate to get through to her but not knowing how. He didn't know how to deal with this kind of fear and anger. This kind of love.

"I will call Jewel's friend, Deputy Rawlings. He will find out the truth." Rage and fear boiled up in her eyes again. "But I already know it. You stole my Maria!"

For an instant, his brain still too sluggish, all Ryder could absorb was what she'd named the baby.

"Maria," he said softly, trying it out. "Maria. It fits."

He wasn't sure what happened next. Or why. But he knew her expression changed. She took a half step back, cocked her head at an angle as she studied him. He didn't know what he looked like, but judging by the soreness of his face, it wasn't pretty. He was confused when he realized that the suspicion, the accusation had faded from her eyes. All he'd done was repeat what she'd named her baby.

He shook his head, trying to clear away the fog. Pain jabbed from his jaw up to his left temple, effectively sharpening his thoughts.

"I didn't take her—" He stopped, grimaced, before adding, "I don't even know your name."

"Nor I yours," she pointed out sharply, clearly not pleased with the distraction from the matter at hand.

"Ryder," he said. "Ryder Grady." He was at least thinking clearly enough not to say "Colton," not here in a house on Bar None land, run by a woman named Jewel who was connected to his brother, by business and by blood.

Means she's connected to you, too, a small voice in the back of his battered brain said, but he shoved it aside.

After a moment, the woman finally returned the nicety, albeit tersely. "Ana Morales. Why should I believe you did not steal her? No one else even knew she was here."

Ana. He tried it out in his mind, aware that if he'd spoken it aloud his voice would likely have held the same wondering tone as Maria had.

"Everybody in this house knew," he said.

"Children," she said with a wave of dismissal. "You accuse children?"

"There are adults here, too." He was finding it a bit easier to talk, now that he was upright and not lying on his ribs.

"Jewel? Macy? You think to blame them for this?"

"I'm not blaming them. Or anyone here. I'm just saying…it's natural they would talk. A new baby, delivered here at the ranch, they would talk. And anyone could have overheard them."

Ana Morales frowned at that. He could see that she was considering his words. For all her justifiable emotional upheaval, she was still thinking. He was grateful for that; otherwise she'd probably be hammering him with those small, hard fists. He knew her strength too well from that night, and didn't doubt he'd have paid a price had she kept coming.

"Ana," he said, "I'm working with the government on this. I know who has her."

She went very still. "You are the police?"

"I'm more of a...private contractor."

"What does that mean?"

"It means I knew some of the men involved. They approached me to help."

She studied him for a moment. "And what do you get in return?"

He winced inwardly. It was the kind of thing he himself would ask, and he wondered what had happened in her young life to make her so cynical. Funny, it seemed only normal to him, but in her, it bothered him.

She wound up pregnant and alone in a strange country, and you're wondering what made her cynical? he asked himself.

But he knew better than to lie to her. Not now, when her emotions were in full flood and her maternal instincts roaring; he sensed she'd know it instantly.

"It was a deal," he admitted, afraid if he told her the rest, she'd never believe him about anything else. "But that doesn't change the facts. I know who has her, Ana. And I can get her back."

"Why should I believe you?" she asked again.

Ryder let out a compressed breath. Even that simple act caused his bruised ribs to ache. And that added pain made him snap, "How about because I trekked halfway across freaking Texas, like this, to tell you?"

He knew he sounded like a petulant child, wanting credit for one of the few noble things he'd ever done in his life, but he didn't care. He was tired, he hurt all over, he thought a couple of those ribs might in fact be cracked, and he wanted nothing more than to lie down and sleep for a week.

"What happened to you?"

He frowned, which hurt nearly as much as a deep breath. "Told you. I tried to stop them."

"And they did this to you? If you work for the government, do you not have a gun?"

"I did. They had more."

And one was aimed at Maria, by a man who wouldn't hesitate to use it, he added silently. He wondered at himself for a moment. He knew instinctively that that, of all the things he could tell her, would stir her to his side. But he couldn't tell her, and he didn't quite understand why.

She would completely lose it, he told himself.

He even believed that. If he told her how close her baby had come to death, she might be unable to function, and right now he needed her thinking hard. It had nothing to do with protecting her—he had never cared about any woman enough to worry about that—nothing at all.

"They?" she finally asked, looking him up and down.

"Four of them," he said, strangely unwilling to let her think he'd been beaten by merely one or two. Thinking his brain must be scrambled, he strove to take charge. Time was wasting and the trail was getting colder by the second. "I need a phone. I have to call my—" He hesitated on the word *handler.* "My contact," he said instead.

She hesitated.

"Ana, please. The longer we wait, the less chance we have of finding Maria."

Again, her daughter's name seemed to turn the tide. "Jewel gave me a cell phone when Maria was born, in case of emergencies," she said, and walked quickly to the dresser and dug into an outside pocket on a large canvas bag. Pink, Ryder noticed, girly again.

She handed it to him. He checked the phone readout for the number. At this hour chances were he'd have to wait for a call back, he explained to Ana. He dialed, keyed in his code and the cell number, then disconnected.

"How long?" she asked.

"A few minutes has been the longest, before."

She stood for a moment, rubbing her arms with her hands as if she were chilled, despite the hot August night. Ryder felt the ridiculous urge to hold her, to take her in his arms and warm her with his own heat, to comfort her…

He even took a step toward her, stopping only when he realized the foolishness of the thought, and realized he was in no shape to comfort anyone.

"Wait here," Ana said, and turned.

Was she going to call for help anyway? "Ana, don't—"

She waved him to silence. "I will not do what you are thinking. There is a first aid box in the children's bathroom."

He'd asked her to trust him, so he guessed he had to trust her as well. He let her go. He heard the distant sound of water running. Moments later she was back, with a wet washcloth, a large towel, and a well-stocked plastic case of bandages, antiseptics and various other implements. He supposed that was a necessity with lots of active kids running around. He should be grateful.

He'd thought she would simply hand it to him and leave it at that, but instead she directed him to sit on the edge of the bed. He did, warily, the movement tugging on bruised rib muscles. He bit back a grunt of pain, telling himself he had no right to complain about a few twinges, not here in this room where she had gone through such agony to bring her baby into the world.

The intimacy of the memories unsettled him.

She began to work without comment, and he noticed with a little surprise that she'd used warm water on the washcloth; he'd expected the shock of cold. Or maybe it was just August in Texas, he thought wryly, and the water never really did get cold.

She was amazingly gentle, her touch soft and compassionate. It still hurt, but he did his best not to show it. When he couldn't manage that, she apologized. He sat there for what seemed like endless minutes, his awareness gradually shifting from the pain to her closeness, and another sort of forced intimacy was suddenly upon him.

She leaned toward him to reach his split lip with the warm cloth. Her breast brushed his arm, and while she didn't react, it took all his focus for him not to jump. An image shot through his mind, of the picture she'd made, sitting in that rocking chair by the window, nursing Maria. In the late-night hour and the privacy of her room, she hadn't covered up, and he'd known even then that he would remember the sight for the rest of his life, the baby's tiny fists kneading that soft, generous curve.

As she moved again, he realized that even through his bloodied nose he could smell a faint scent of soap or shampoo.

Had she been out on a date?

The idea made him frown, which made her apologize. He let it go; he certainly didn't want to explain that it was his thought, not pain, that had caused the expression.

But then a vague, hazy memory came to him, of lying outside her window, safe in the shadows of the house, and hearing first the ranch's van, then the excited laughter of children for a brief moment before the garage door had settled heavily into place.

She'd been out with the children, not a man. And he didn't like how relieved that made him.

"This needs stitches," she said as she swabbed at the most painful spot, on his left temple, about even with his eyebrow.

"It'll keep. Just use those," he said, gesturing at the small packet of butterfly bandages in the first aid kit.

To his surprise she didn't argue with him, just did as he asked. Then he realized he shouldn't be surprised; she was likely only doing this to keep herself distracted when everything in her must be screaming to go after her baby.

It hit him, the enormity of the trust she had put in him. He didn't know if it had been the weight of his government connection, or if she simply trusted him to help her as he had the night Maria was born. It was hard to believe that much faith could be built in so short a time, but he had to admit it had been transforming even for him.

And if it convinced her...

"Your ribs are hurt," she said.

He grimaced. "My dramatic exit was a bit...costly."

He explained to her how he'd faked a fall into the gully, and played dead when they'd peered over at him. He didn't say it was likely the only reason he was still alive, but he saw in her eyes that he didn't have to; she might be young, but she wasn't a fool. He hadn't mistaken the keen intelligence there.

"Take off your shirt."

He blinked. Then connected it, belatedly and feeling foolish, to her comment about his ribs.

"There's nothing to do about them."

"But you are bleeding there as well. It should be cleaned, stopped. You will do Maria no good if you collapse."

She had a point. He took off his shirt. And closed his eyes, telling himself it was so she couldn't see the flash of pain in his eyes, not so that he could concentrate on the feel of her fingers on his bare skin.

The stupidity of such thoughts when he was hurting so much, when there was so much at stake, wasn't lost on him, and he made a fierce effort to regain his focus.

The cell phone rang. He stared at it for a split second, disconcerted by the ring. She'd obviously programmed it for the baby, a quiet, simple lullaby. Recovering, he grabbed it, checked the readout and answered.

Thankfully, it was Gibson and not Furnell.

He explained quickly, leaving out his personal connection to the baby. They didn't need to know. Better that they didn't; if they thought he had a personal stake in this, they might pull him off the mission.

"Why didn't you just play along?" Gibson asked.

Clearly, instead of mooning over Ana, he should have been thinking of answers to questions he should have known were coming. He could hardly explain it all now.

"It just went haywire," he said. "Alcazar's main man, he decided he didn't trust me."

Gibson's voice was suddenly sharp. "Did they know you were working for us?"

"I don't think so. The guy just didn't like me. Maybe he thought I was trying to move in on his spot."

It was lame, but the best he could come up with. Quickly he went on, hoping Gibson would drop the questions he couldn't answer for the moment.

"I don't know where they were taking her. We were supposed to get a call with further directions."

"A cell call?"

"Probably." Something else occurred to him. "They told me I'd be driving back the way I came. First cell reception should be about at the west corner of the Bar None where it meets the county road. It drops to next to nothing after that."

"Hold on." There was a minute or two of dead air, and Ryder wondered if they had a way to check on any cell calls made in the area.

They're the feds—of course they do. What good would they be if they didn't?

"Three calls around the right time," Gibson said without preamble when he came back. "One from a local prefix, two with Del Rio prefixes."

Ryder went still. "The limo, the one Alcazar was in when we met up…it had one of those metal logos attached. Some dealer in Del Rio."

"Right on the border," Gibson said. "That could be the start of their network. We may have been looking in the wrong place for that end of the operation."

Ryder spoke quickly, before the man could bolt too far in that direction, away from where Ryder needed him to focus.

"We've got to find that baby," he said. "She's our best chance at breaking up this end of the ring."

"She?" the agent asked.

Ryder ignored the curiosity. "We've never been this close before, Gibson."

If the agent was surprised by Ryder's unaccustomed use of his name, he didn't let on. "I know. We've never been on them this soon after they've picked up a kid."

It's not some anonymous kid, Ryder shouted in his mind. It's Maria, damn it!

"They'll be moving her for a while yet, if we're right about how far they like to get from the border before they hand off to the next link."

"We are," Gibson said. "You know we've been working this from the other end, too."

Ryder knew they had, that they had located at least three couples who had obtained their babies through this operation. The last he'd heard, none of them had been very cooperative, fearing the loss of the child they considered their own.

Bought and paid for, Ryder thought sourly.

Did they ever think about the parents, the mothers like Ana, grieving endlessly?

He knew that wasn't quite fair, that the couples were likely told by the operators of the ring that the children were discards, unwanted, that they were giving them a much better life than they would otherwise have had. And maybe in some cases it was true.

But not in Maria's.

"Have you gotten anything out of them?"

"Not yet. But we think one of the men is about to break. I'll let you know."

"Immediately," Ryder said, not caring if Gibson took offense at being ordered by his ex-con recruit. But Gibson sounded more amused than offended.

"Those Del Rio calls have to be the right ones," Ryder said. "Can you track them back, isolate the phones they came from, and track those?"

"Maybe, if I can commandeer the resources. Sit tight, I'll be in touch. This number?"

"Yes," Ryder said, not explaining that he meant only to the last part; he had no intention of sitting tight and waiting. Not when Ana had put her trust in him.

Not when he had promised a tiny little girl that he would bring her back to her mother.

Chapter 13

Ana set her jaw.

"No."

She said it firmly. She had somehow found the backbone to face down her father, and her fiancé. She had had the courage to sneak out when they'd tried to confine her. She'd had the nerve to make her way on the perilous path out of her country to a different, strange, wonderful yet frightening place where she was determined to make a new life for herself and her baby.

She certainly was not going to back down now just because this man had told her to stay here and let him handle this. She was through blindly trusting the men in her life to do the right thing.

She had put her trust in this man, that was true.

But not blindly.

"Ana, you can't. You need to stay here, wait for me to—"

"I will not."

"It's only been two weeks since Maria was born. You can't go chasing off—"

"I am fine. And that is for me to decide."

"These are dangerous men."

She glanced at the bloody washcloth she had used to clean his face, his ribs, then met his gaze.

"Do you truly think I do not know this?"

"That's not what I meant."

"They have my baby," Ana said simply, as if there was nothing else to be said.

And for her, that was true.

Ryder studied her for a long, silent moment. She returned his gaze levelly, masking her instinctive sympathetic response to his battered face. And hiding the unwanted appreciation she was feeling for the beautiful way this man was put together. Hard and lean, not soft like Alberto. Just looking at his bare chest made her feel odd longings, made her wonder what it would feel like pressed against her.

She wished he would put his shirt back on.

She was not unaware that, if he was telling her the truth, he had already sacrificed a great deal for Maria. But her past experience had taught her the value of that simple word *if.*

"I appreciate what you have done," she began, then stopped when a sardonic expression flitted across his face.

"If I'd done what I should have," he said as he did as she'd silently wished and pulled his bloodied shirt back on, "I'd have been bringing Maria home to you, not just dragging my own sorry ass here."

The bitterness in his voice startled her, and despite her doubts, she found she believed that it was genuine. He truly blamed himself for not rescuing her baby right then, outnumbered or not.

She still had reservations, and deep inside she feared she might regret going against her better judgment, but her judgment had told her for too long to ignore the obvious about her father, and then about Alberto.

"You say you can find her."

"I've never been so close to cracking the ring. Never known when they had…a baby in the pipeline, only found out afterward. This is the time, when the pathway they've built is in use."

Ana listened. It made sense. But when it came down to it, much as she might hate the idea of what these men were doing, only one thing mattered to her.

"I do not care about them. I cannot afford to care about them. I care only about Maria."

"Then stay here, and stay safe for her."

"I have decided to trust you, Ryder," she said, using his name for the first time since he'd given it to her. "But I am not a fool. I believe a great man in this country once said 'Trust, but verify.' I intend to follow that advice."

"Ana—"

She held up a hand to stop his protest. "I made a promise to my little girl. I promised her that I would build a new life, a better life for her, that I would never give up on that dream. And I will not."

Ryder was looking at her with a touch of amazement, which puzzled her. She did not find what she was saying so strange, or different. It was what any true, loving parent would do, was it not?

"And besides," she said, "you are injured. You may need help."

He lifted a dark brow, then winced at the movement. Ana managed not to react to this obvious sign proving of her point, but his wry grimace told her he had gotten it.

"And I may be of use in other ways," she added. "Women can sometimes go unnoticed where a man cannot."

He blinked, looking startled this time. "I suppose."

She pressed her case. "I am coming with you," she said firmly. "The only question is how much energy you will waste in trying to stop me."

She saw the moment when he gave up. Without a word she turned and began to gather some few items that she tucked into the pink bag that had served her as a diaper bag but carried all the other baby accoutrements as well, plus her own small store of things she would ordinarily put in a handbag.

"What are you doing? You want to lug all that?"

She looked over her shoulder. "This is the trusting part. You say you will find Maria, so I will need her things."

Were it not for her deep, gnawing fear for her little girl, the look on his face, even through the swelling on his jaw and around his eye would have made her smile.

Ryder felt a little like he'd been caught up in a tornado. Or maybe a flash flood. There was no stopping either, and there was obviously no stopping Ana Morales.

He thought about slipping out now, starting out on his own, while she was changing clothes in the bathroom. But he had the distinct feeling that if he did, she would merely follow him anyway. And he would rather have her where he could keep an eye on her than out poking into dangerous territory by herself.

Which, he thought ruefully, is exactly what she'd do.

He shook his aching head, but cautiously. He sat there, trying not to imagine what she looked like, shedding one set of clothes for another. How had this woman, in such a short time, become the focus of his world? He'd already admitted the obvious, that she was a strikingly beautiful—

and clearly intelligent—woman. And that he admired her determination wasn't so hard to acknowledge. That he was slightly in awe of this kind of fierce, maternal love, was a bit harder, but he couldn't deny it.

He was having trouble with the realization that the combination made him incredibly, ridiculously hot. Beautiful, sure. That was always a plus, although it hadn't always been a requirement. But the rest? Hadn't he always shied away from smart, determined women? The kind who wouldn't settle for the little he was able—or willing—to give?

Or was it just that you knew they wouldn't have anything to do with you? That any woman with smarts would see right through you?

That little voice in his head was starting to annoy him. He'd never been troubled by it before, and didn't think it was a coincidence that it had started nagging him shortly after he'd been stupid enough to let Boots get to him. The old man had a lot to answer for, and Ryder was going to let him know it when this was all over. With no small amount of pleasure.

Ana came back, dressed in a pair of black jeans and a sleeveless black turtleneck. The clothes made her look impossibly slender for a woman who had just given birth two weeks ago. Yet the full swell of her breasts and the womanly curve of her hips reminded him, as if he'd needed any reminder.

In one hand she carried a lightweight jacket. In the other, puzzlingly, she had a glass of water.

She held the glass out to him. He took it, looking at her curiously. Then she held out a small bottle that had been hidden by the glass.

Aspirin, he realized.

"Bless you," he said, meaning it, and powered down four in a hurry.

"Take them with us," she said. "There are children's aspirin for the little ones."

He'd already planned on it, and stuffed the bottle into a pocket. He was going to welcome the relief they gave him before this was over.

"I'll need to keep your phone."

She nodded without comment.

"They took my truck," he said. "We're going to need a vehicle."

"There is a truck here. Besides the van Jewel drives. She said I could use it any time."

It seemed she had a answer for everything. "They took my gun, too. I don't suppose there's a weapon in this place?"

"With all the children?"

"It's Texas," he countered.

"Jewel would never take the chance." Then, after a moment, she added, "I am sure there would be weapons over at the Colton ranch."

She didn't, he knew, realize the jolt she'd just given him. But she was sharp, and quick, and he didn't want her to guess, so he muttered, "I don't think so," and turned away.

I can just see myself, knocking on Clay's door. "Hey, bro, yeah, I'm out, and just when you thought you were rid of me for good, here I am. And by the way, I need to borrow your scattergun…"

No, the Bar None was not an option. Not that he wouldn't be above sneaking in and grabbing what he needed from the gun rack, but Clay had never been a sound sleeper—all that worrying and responsibility—and Ryder didn't want to risk it.

Wouldn't risk it.

The last thing he wanted right now was to have to explain himself and what he was up to to his brother. Clay would likely never believe him anyway. Clay had washed his hands of his irresponsible, troublesome little brother when he'd gotten into the scrape that had landed him here, and Ryder didn't blame him.

At the sound of a drawer sliding shut Ryder snapped out of his reverie, annoyed that anything had the power to take his mind off the crisis at hand. More to lay at Boots's door, he thought. The old man had harped on him endlessly about mending the breach between him and Clay. That had to be what had him thinking about even an unpleasant confrontation, when before he would have laughed off the idea before the image even formed.

Apparently he hadn't quite succeeded in cutting himself off completely, at least not in his mind.

You can't ever pry your family out of your heart, boy. No matter how hard you try.

He'd laughed at Boots then. "Maybe not, but you can freeze them out," he'd said, knowing it was true, because he'd done it.

Assuming he had a heart to begin with, of course.

"I have this, if you wish it."

He turned, and his eyes widened as he saw what Ana Morales held out to him.

It was a knife.

But not just some small, useless, ladylike pocketknife.

This was a blade. In a tooled leather sheath, it looked to be at least six inches long, with the hilt adding another four. And what a hilt it was; some dark, exotic-looking wood carved into curves to perfectly fit the hand that gripped it, and inlaid with something white and gleaming that had the sheen of pearls. The butt end of the hilt was set with what looked for all the world like a real ruby; it winked blood red in the light.

Almost in awe, he reached out and took it. He slid the knife out of the sheath. The grip seemed a little small to him, but the polished blade of clearly fine steel glinted. A quick touch with his thumb told him it was honed to the kind of fine edge that had given rise to the expression "splitting hairs."

The knife was meant for damage, the tip a fine point for stabbing, and the deadly curve that came after for slicing with ease.

And it had to be worth a lot, he thought, knowing instinctively that this was something a collector would prize. It was an elegant, almost dashing kind of weapon, and the old-fashioned word didn't seem silly as he held the perfectly balanced knife.

"Where in the hell did you get this?"

"It was my great-great-great-grandmother's."

He blinked. That explained the size of the grip, then. "Your great-great-great-grandmother?"

"That is correct? The mother of my mother's mother's mother's mother?"

He wasn't even going to try to work that one out. "Close enough," he said. "It's beautiful."

Ana smiled, the first he'd seen from her tonight. The first he'd seen from her since the moment he'd handed her her baby.

"My great-great-great-grandfather did not think it so beautiful. She tried to kill him with it, the first time they met. She tells of it in her journal, which was handed down to me."

He stared at her. A smile of his own started to curve his mouth; she'd come by that courage and nerve honestly, it seemed. Whatever he'd thought about her when he'd first seen her, the idea that she was simply another illegal in a long line had vanished now. There was much more to this woman than he knew. This little bit of her history proved that.

He wanted to hear that story about her great-whatever grandmother, but he knew there wasn't time.

He wanted to hear all her stories.

The realization jolted him even more than the sound of the name Colton coming from her had. He wanted to know everything about her, what had made her the incredible woman she was. He wanted it all, and he had never wanted to know such things about a woman. He never wanted to know anything beyond what he needed to figure out how to get her into bed.

He told himself that he was thinking this way because he knew that was not an option, given the short time since Maria's birth. It was a comforting theory, but he wasn't sure he believed it. Because he still wanted to know everything about her.

But the first thing he was going to need to know, he thought, was the most important.

Was she running to this country simply for a better life, or was she escaping something unbearable in her old life? And what—or who—was it?

Then the thing that was truly the most important belatedly hit him. Whoever or whatever it was…was it coming after her?

Chapter 14

It was right, Ana thought, that her ancestor's gleaming weapon be used in this hunt. She knew in her heart that Elena Maria de la Costa would approve; she would count no cost too high for family. That it was a great-times-three granddaughter would make no difference; blood was blood, and you took care of your own.

Unless and until they betrayed you.

She had wondered if the ancestor she most admired, would have been ashamed of her for what she'd done, for leaving her father and the father of her child.

More likely, for being fool enough to be taken in by them in the first place.

But then she had gone back to that treasured diary, read again the tales of an older time, and of the spirited life Elena had led, and what she had thought of what went on around her. Elena's true character, bold and smart and fearless, had shone through the pages, and as she had since the first time she had read those pages as a girl, Ana felt as if she'd known this long-ago woman who was forever linked to her.

And she realized that Elena Maria de la Costa would have understood.

And probably would have sliced Alberto before she left, Ana had thought then.

Like Ryder was about to slice the man whose throat he had under Elena's blade now. The man who had been so obviously stunned to see Ryder when he had pulled him out of the car parked behind the roadhouse tavern.

"You're dead!" he'd exclaimed then.

"Exaggerated claim," Ryder had said smoothly as he'd searched the man for weapons, jamming the lethal-looking handgun he found in the man's waistband under his shirt into his own belt.

Ana's reaction hadn't been so calm. The man's words told her Ryder's story had been the truth; he had tried to save Maria and they had killed him for it.

Or rather, thought they had.

The tentative trust she had put in him got a bit more solid in that moment. And she felt an odd ache inside, over and above her worry for Maria, an ache at the idea that this man had risked his very life for her little girl. She wished to reach out and touch him, to thank him, but now was not the time.

Nor was it time to follow the other, unexpected and unlikely urge she felt; kissing this man would be intriguing, she was sure, but hardly appropriate just now.

Instead, she studied this thing—she hesitated to call him a man—who had helped steal her little girl. She found her fingers curling, wishing it was she who held her ancestor's blade to his scrawny throat.

"You can talk to me now," Ryder was saying, "or I can see that you never talk again."

"I tell you, I don't know!"

"Then you're no use to me, are you?" He shifted, as if in preparation for that fatal slice of the blade. The man screeched.

"If I knew, I'd tell you!"

Ryder seemed to consider this. He glanced her way. She saw the question in his eyes, as if he were asking her if she was satisfied this was the truth. But there was something more there, an uneasiness it took her a moment to understand.

He expected her to be horrified by what he was doing.

She nearly laughed; if only he knew the anger she harbored, the craving to punish this man and all his partners in these heinous acts.

The craving to slaughter, painfully, the man who dared lay his hands on her little girl.

"I mean what I said," she told Ryder softly. "I will stop at nothing. *Nothing.*"

The man under the blade was watching this exchange, bewilderment on his face.

"Who is this bitch? Who the hell are *you?*"

"Me? I'm the guy you killed back there in that gully, remember?"

The man looked at him warily. He scoffed, but there was a touch of uncertainty in his voice. Did he truly believe he was looking at a ghost? Ana wondered. Then she realized he was drunk enough that his thought processes were tangled. If they were ever clear, she thought, reminding herself again of what this man had done, what he did to make his money.

And she, who had been a gentle loving child, thought

she would relish nothing more than to see this man's throat laid open like a filleted trout.

"You some kind of cop after all?"

"You'll never know," Ryder whispered, and shifted the gleaming blade.

The man screamed, broke.

"I swear," he babbled, choking out the words as if fear were throttling him, "I don't know anything. I got my orders from Duane, I just did what he told me. I just rode shotgun on the first leg, mostly, I never handled any of the brats. I hate 'em."

"Who took the next leg?"

Ryder shifted the blade again, and Ana saw blood begin to trickle down the man's unshaven neck. Funny how the stubble of beard looked simply unkempt on this man, but had looked oddly attractive on Ryder that night. Even then she'd wanted to touch, to feel the stubble rasp against her fingers. Another urge that was unexpected and startling.

Right now, of course, his face was still swollen and reddened from the beating he'd taken. The beating he'd taken for her little girl.

Yet he was still a very attractive man. Even now.

Perhaps even more attractive now, she thought. Now, when he was so fiercely intent on the mission, on finding Maria.

The trust she had put in him suddenly shifted form, as unwanted emotion slipped into the mix, making her nervously aware that she was letting things get confused in her mind and heart.

That way lay disaster, and she tried to quash the feeling. She would focus on nothing but the search, think of this man as nothing more than the best tool she had at hand to use to find her daughter.

"Marco," the man finally gasped out, believing at last

that Ryder would do what he threatened. "He lives in the motel, east end of Esperanza."

Ryder didn't back off a millimeter. "Room?"

"Nine."

Ryder moved quickly then, using the man's own belt to fasten his hands tightly behind him. He instructed Ana to find the trunk release on the car. She leaned into the vehicle, her nose crinkling at the smell of stale food she couldn't see, and the faint odor of urine. She found the latch labeled with a drawing of an open trunk, and pulled it.

Ryder searched the trunk first, thoroughly, and after pulling out the spare tire to look beneath, handed her a box of ammunition, which she assumed was for the gun the man carried.

"I don't want him warning anyone. Any problem with leaving him here?" he asked as he dumped the protesting man into his own trunk.

"Only that he is still alive," Ana said bluntly.

Ryder chuckled. "He may not be, if no one finds him by tomorrow morning. It's August in Texas, and it probably gets hot enough you could roast a chicken in there."

"That would be justice," she said.

The man looked at her as if he realized she was the biggest threat. "Who are you?" he wailed, looking at Ana.

"Haven't you guessed?" Ryder said, stuffing a greasy rag he'd found into the man's mouth, thankfully stifling any further wails. "She's an avenging angel, straight from God, and it's judgment day."

He slammed the trunk lid down, cutting off the muffled scream.

"Will you truly leave him there?" Ana asked after they had moved the car. They'd put it in a secluded spot in the strip mall's parking lot, where any sound the man made would likely not be heard, until the world started to wake up again. Ryder had searched until he'd found the man's cell phone, and a check of the number told him this was not one of the Del Rio ones.

"Does it matter?" Ryder asked.

She didn't waste time pondering. "Not really."

"I didn't think so," he said, although he suspected should the man really die, she would feel a qualm of remorse. Ana Morales was a very complex woman, he was beginning to realize.

And a very good one, in an old-fashioned sense of the word he'd never applied to a woman before because it had never mattered. A good woman had never been something he'd hankered for; give him a party girl, out for fun, with no strings, every time.

He'd go back to that, he assured himself. As soon as this was over, and Maria was back with her mother and these scumbags were where they belonged. He'd finish his job, break the ring, and go on about his life with a clean record. No need to get too drastic about changing. He'd just be smarter this time.

"I'll call my contacts, eventually," he said. "Tell them where he is."

He didn't explain that he couldn't call them now, because they likely would try to rein him in, tell him to wait until they had agents in place. They might even pull him off altogether, now that things seemed to be on the verge of breaking loose.

And there was no way he was letting anyone pull him off this now. Not until he had personally put that baby back in Ana's arms.

An image of what that would be like shot through his

mind, of seeing that tiny bundle safely back with her mother, of the joyous expression that would spread across Ana's face. It made him smile, even though it hurt his split lip.

"You are smiling," she said into the darkness of the truck cab.

"I was thinking of your smile, when you have your baby back."

He didn't know why he'd admitted that. Something about this woman seemed to make him run at the mouth.

When she spoke, her words were soft. "You are a good man, Ryder."

That pronouncement, coming from a woman like Ana Morales, nearly made him laugh. But he couldn't bring himself to correct her. He didn't want her knowing just how wrong she was. He'd never really cared before, had known his bad-boy reputation attracted exactly the kind of woman he preferred, but this was different.

Everything with this woman was different.

When she reached out and gently put a hand on his arm as he drove, he just about jumped out of his skin.

"Thank you," she said quietly.

"I haven't found her yet."

"But you will. I believe that."

As he slowed for a turn he glanced at her. She was watching him with a steady look that stabbed through to his soul as surely as if she'd used her blade on him.

This was a woman who'd have your back. Forever.

He nearly jumped again as he realized he'd actually thought the word *forever* in relation to a woman. But as he stared at her, feeling somehow bigger, stronger under the unwavering gaze of her dark eyes, he realized she was a woman who deserved nothing less.

Marco was sound asleep when Ryder rousted him out

after silently and easily breaking into the seedy motel room. It seemed clear that he was not living high on the proceeds of the smuggling ring, but then, that was typical. Alcazar drove a limo, the peons lived in dives like this.

Marco was even more astonished to see Ryder alive. And thankfully for Ryder's rapidly diminishing patience—he was hurting, damn it, and thanks to these bastards he had to grit his teeth and keep going—he broke much more easily.

"Denny," the man sputtered. "That's who you need."

"Please," Ryder said scornfully. "The guy you relegated to driving because you think he's too stupid for anything else?"

Even as he said it, Ryder remembered that it was Denny who had figured out he had some connection to Maria. Perhaps he'd underestimated the man. But he didn't think he'd misjudged his colleague's opinion of him.

"That's just it," Marco said, eyeing the knife Ana was now holding even more warily than the commandeered handgun Ryder held. There was something about a woman with a knife that made some men very nervous. He'd been there himself a time or two, where if the woman of the moment could have laid her hands on a blade he probably would have been minus some body parts he was exceptionally fond of.

"What's just it?" Ryder prompted.

"He's the one who drove. He always drove."

It hit him then, belatedly. Of course. If Denny drove, then he knew where they'd gone.

"Where is he?"

"At this hour? At home, I guess." When Ana shifted the knife in her grip and took a step toward him, the man scrabbled back in the bed like a frightened crab. "He lives behind the church, over on Boone Street."

The irony of that bit deep as Ryder grabbed a belt from the back of a chair. With it, he found some nylon shoelaces freed from a pair of worn shoes on the floor by the bed and tied the man up. He crossed the room to a small closet, searched it, then shoved the man inside and closed the door.

He searched the small apartment until he found another handgun and a cell phone—again not one of the ones with the Del Rio prefix—and took both. There was a landline phone on a table, and when he indicated it, Ana quickly severed the cord with her knife.

With a certain amount of relish, Ryder thought.

He smiled inwardly at the memory of Marco's expression when he'd seen this gloriously angry woman contemplating him with that lethal blade in her hand.

"I wonder," he mused aloud as they headed toward Boone Street, "if he thinks living behind a church means some salvation will seep into him."

"If so, he is a fool."

"The rest of them would agree with you that he's stupid," Ryder said. "But I'm not so sure. He's the one who figured out I...knew Maria."

He felt more than saw her gaze sharpen, something about the way she turned slightly toward him in the passenger seat of the truck, and then went very still and quiet.

"I am sorry I doubted you."

He wasn't sure what had brought on the change of heart. Perhaps she'd sensed that he'd been more than willing to follow through on his threat, if it would help them find Maria. The realization had startled him; for all his sins he'd never been one to treat human life lightly. Nevertheless, he knew it was true.

What he didn't know was why. And it was too big of a

tangle, sitting somewhere south of his heart near his gut, for him to try and sort out now.

As they pulled up to a stoplight—he didn't want to risk attracting any attention, even though the streets of little Esperanza were deserted at this hour—he flicked her a sideways glance. "You just keep right on doubting me, and everyone. Until you have your baby back."

After a moment she gave a short, sharp nod.

When they got to the small apartment above the garage behind the picturesque white clapboard building with the traditional steeple, there was a light on inside. At least, he thought there was; it seemed faint, and flickered oddly. A fire? Surely not, not in August. And not in this little place, that he doubted very much had any kind of a fireplace.

Unless it was…a fire.

Ryder tensed. This guy was their best lead, and Ryder wasn't about to let him toast himself before he talked.

He gauged the strength of the door; the building was old, and the paint on the door and the jamb was weathered, peeling. There was no lock other than the one in the doorknob, no dead bolt visible, something Ryder found odd for a man in his kind of business.

His final assessment was that he could probably take it down with one good hit. He didn't want to think what the effort would do to his already bruised body, but there was no other option. There were no balconies near the two windows, no other possible access points that he could see. He pulled the weapon he'd liberated from Marco free of his belt, then motioned Ana to stand back so he could back up on the landing for a running start.

"It is locked?" she whispered.

The man was apparently the main driver on the network

that smuggled stolen babies, Ryder thought, and whispered back, "Of course it's…"

His voice trailed away as he thought of all the times in his life when he'd overlooked the obvious. Tentatively he reached out and tested the knob.

It turned. Easily.

He gave her a sheepish look, but she didn't seem inclined to be critical. She merely nodded and waited.

But she had her three-times-great-grandmother's knife in her hand.

If I were the man who had her baby, I'd be a hell of a lot more worried about her than me, Ryder thought.

He backed to one side of the door, motioned her behind him, and when she'd moved, he reached out and turned the knob.

The door creaked open like the sound effects from some old spooky movie. Great burglar alarm. Maybe that was why he didn't bother with new locks. Nobody'd sneak through that door.

Nothing happened.

"Candles," Ana whispered, so close no one more than six inches away could have heard her. Her breath brushed warmly over his ear.

Ryder suppressed a shiver, and suddenly, inanely, realized the truth of the old joke, "Blow in my ear and I'll follow you anywhere."

But then he caught the scent that had made her say it, a sweet, warm aroma that reminded him of a woman in Amarillo, who had always wanted candles burning when they had sex. Which in turn reminded him that he hadn't thought that way of another woman since he'd met Ana, a realization that only furthered that tangle in his gut.

Get on with it, he told himself.

He inched forward, weapon at the ready, safety off, a round chambered. He didn't want to kill the guy before he talked, but he didn't want to die, either.

He made a quick, sharp move with his head, just enough to get a glimpse into the room. Ana had been right. Candles, a small row of them, were burning on a low table near the center of the room. They were also the only light in the room, which made it difficult to see into the shadowy corners. He'd have to—

He froze as he heard a sound from inside. Footsteps. His grip on the Mac 10 tightened.

Then there was a rustling, a slight thump, as if of something hitting the floor.

The voice that came out of the darkness startled him. But the words shocked him even more.

"I've been waiting for you. Come in."

Chapter 15

Denny was the only one who hadn't been surprised to see him alive.

In fact, he wasn't surprised to see him at all.

"You knew I wasn't dead," Ryder said.

"I knew."

"How?"

"Call it...instinct. Marco and the others, they have seen one or two dead men. I've seen enough to smell death."

"But you didn't tell them."

The man shrugged. "They don't care much for my opinion. And they figured if you weren't you would be soon enough, banged up as you were. Coyotes, cougars, something would have finished you off." He flashed an interested look at Ryder's battered face. "Obviously they underestimated you."

Ryder shifted his grip on the pistol. Denny was sitting—or rather kneeling—on the floor in front of the table that held the bank of candles. The thump he'd heard, he guessed. There was no weapon in evidence, but he doubted the man would have it in plain sight. He'd told Ana to wait outside until he assessed the odd situation, and so far, she was doing as he asked. But he also doubted she would stay there for long.

Just as he was doubting that this man was as stupid as his co-conspirators thought he was.

"So," he said casually, "how's the dumb-as-a-brick act working for you?"

For an instant, something flickered in the man's eyes. Or maybe it was the candlelight, making him look as if he were smiling.

"Are you after the baby, or the network?" The man asked it as if he were a salesclerk asking a customer which product he preferred.

"Yes," Ryder said, then added, "in that order."

The smile was real this time, then the man gave the barest of nods. "I suspected as much. Is it yours?"

"No," Ryder said. And then, he added the most important qualifier. "And yes."

Denny tilted his head sideways, in the same way he had when he'd been pondering Ryder's reaction to seeing Maria. As he thought of her name, Ryder realized with a little shock he hadn't even known it then.

Ryder wasn't even sure why he was talking to this man, as if there were some kind of rational discussion to be had, as if this were a civilized conversation instead of a dangerous meeting about a despicable act.

"I presume you already found Marco and Carl?"

"Yes."

Denny nodded again. "I'm guessing Marco directed you here?"

Again with the politeness, Ryder thought, on the edge of losing patience with this whole charade.

"If you want to call it *directed*," he snapped out.

"Are they dead?"

"Not yet," Ryder said, deciding it might be wise to take out a little insurance. Not that he expected any of these scumbags to particularly care if another died, beyond some blow to their pride. "But if I don't make some calls by morning, it's a definite possibility."

Again Denny seemed to ponder this, and apparently decided he believed him. At least, once more he nodded.

At this point, Ryder had no idea how this was going to go. Wasn't even sure how to approach this lowlife with the odd demeanor.

And then it was taken out of his hands, as Ana walked through the door, bared blade glinting in her hand. Denny's head came up and, as he looked at Ana, his eyes widened speculatively. And then filled with understanding, as if it had all been explained to him.

"This is taking too much time," she said, eyeing the man, first with suspicion, then with comprehension. "If you think God will forgive you for a few prayers, you are misguided."

Denny nodded yet again. "How well I know. That—" Ryder tensed as he raised a hand, but Denny only gestured in the general direction of the door "—was my grandfather's church, once."

"Then he would be ashamed of you."

Ryder thought of Boots, wondered what he would make of this, if he would believe in this apparent paroxysm of guilt and repentance.

"I have no doubt he is," Denny said. Then, briskly, "The man you are looking for is Dr. Gary Breither."

"Bingo," Ryder whispered.

He'd long suspected the man, from the moment he'd heard that the notoriously incompetent physician was suddenly doing noticeably better financially. And had been making regular trips south of the border, declaring self-aggrandizingly that he was doing extensive charity work.

Ryder had thought this the perfect cover, and had wondered if the services he'd offered had been to poor, pregnant women, whose babies he had then offered up to the smugglers. But he'd hidden his tracks well—he might be inept as a doctor, but as a financial sneak he was stellar—and even the feds hadn't yet been able to trace his money trail.

Ana, however, was still suspicious. "Why should we believe you, when you give up so easily?"

Denny shrugged. "As you wish."

"Why *did* you give it up so easily?" Ryder asked, for the first time looking at Denny as a man rather than just one of the maggots feeding on the desperation of others.

"I suspect," Denny said, shifting his oddly steady gaze to Ryder, "for much the same reason you nearly threw your life away. Because the package was no longer just a package."

It flashed through Ryder's mind again, that moment when he'd unzipped the bag and realized the baby inside was the same one he'd brought into the world a few days before. Remembered the puzzled, almost bewildered expression that had crossed Denny's face as he worked to figure it out.

And again he thought of Boots. Of everything he'd spoken of, everything he'd tried to teach him. Going with his gut, Ryder slipped the safety back on the purloined Mac 10 and stuffed it back in his belt.

"You believe him?" Ana said, sounding a little startled.

"I do. Let's go."

"We are just going to leave him here? Free to call and warn this doctor?"

"I don't think he will."

"I will not," Denny confirmed.

Ana's hand tightened around the hilt of her knife. She was clearly not willing to trust Ryder's judgment on this.

"But," Denny said, eyeing her with something Ryder would have sworn was appreciation, "you may take my cell phone. It's on the table by the door."

Ryder nodded. Ana gaped at them both. "I do not understand. Why do you trust this man? He was one of the ones who beat you, is he not?"

"I'm not sure he ever really landed a blow. But he's got bigger problems right now. Because he knows—" he gestured at the candles "—that you're right. God won't forgive him, for a few prayers."

"So we are just going to leave him here?"

Again Ryder thought of Boots. "He'll punish himself more than we ever could. Or his God will."

Denny lowered his eyes, focusing on the candles. And Ryder wondered if he would choose to end his torture with a bullet to his head, or spend his life trying to atone, as Boots had.

Either way, Dr. Breither had lost his driver.

Ana wondered briefly if she were a fool for trusting this man, and his judgment about the man they'd just left. She watched him as he drove, studied his profile, the faint shadows of the marks on his skin where the men who had Maria had beaten him. She remembered the marks on his body as well, across that lovely chest and along the ribs above his narrow, flat waist…

The sudden heat embarrassed her. Even though she knew he couldn't see her in the faint light of the truck cab, she lowered her gaze and focused on what truly mattered, what it must be costing him to simply keep going through the pain.

For Maria, she reminded herself. And tried to quash the tiny ache inside, the burgeoning emotions that made her wish it was a little bit for her, too.

They were a couple of blocks from the church when her cell phone rang. Thankful she had changed the ring or she'd be sorting through the pile of phones they had accumulated, she grabbed it.

"It says restricted number," she told Ryder as she handed it to him as he drove, although she knew no one would be calling her at this hour except perhaps Jewel.

She felt a pang. On Ryder's instructions she had left a note saying only that she was well and with a friend, and would be in touch when she could. They had no way of knowing if one of the children had been manipulated into betraying Maria's existence to the smuggling ring.

But Ana knew that despite the note, the woman who had done so much for her would be beyond worried when she found both Ana and Maria gone unexpectedly. Ana had no real friends in the area, she could only hope Jewel would wait before telling anyone.

Ryder answered, listened, said nothing for what seemed like an endless stretch, then said, "Got it," and snapped the phone closed.

"Ryder?" she said when he didn't speak. Surely he wasn't going to refuse to tell her what his contact had said.

"They got the same name," he said after a minute. "Out of one of the couples who paid for a baby they never got."

It hit Ana then, that somewhere perhaps there was a desperate couple who had paid for Maria.

"Despreciable," she muttered.

"Yes, it would be despicable, if they knew," Ryder said. "But these guys are smooth, Ana. They have...well, salesmen on the other end, guys who convince people these are unwanted children, given up voluntarily. Or children who would be abused or abandoned—or worse—if left where they are."

"You are saying these people think they are saving these babies?"

"I can't say they all do, I'm sure some of them suspect it's not all legit, but yes, I think some do."

Ana pondered that for a moment. "I suppose," she said reluctantly, "I can understand someone wanting a baby so much."

Ryder made a sound, a male sort of grunt Ana had learned early in life served as an answer when a man had no answer for you.

"You do not believe in such a great need for a child?"

"I have to believe in it. This smuggling ring wouldn't exist if that need didn't."

"But you...you do not have this need yourself."

He shifted as if uncomfortable. But when he finally answered, she knew she was getting the truth. "No," he said. "I've never had it."

She turned this over and over in her mind, looking for a way to resolve the seeming contradiction. Finally, even knowing he would likely just grunt again, she spoke.

"Yet you risked your life for Maria. You could have died for her."

He did not even grunt. He said nothing. And she realized that she should have put it in the form of a question; another thing she had learned, belatedly, was that men tended to be quite literal, especially when dealing with aspects of emotion.

"Why?" she said, correcting her lapse.

She thought he still might not answer, but at last he said, somewhat lamely, "She's already here."

It made a strange sort of sense, Ana supposed. But she couldn't resist probing further.

"But if you feel nothing for children, why did you—"

"I didn't say I felt nothing. Just that I didn't feel the need to have them myself."

His mouth quirked, and she had the feeling he'd gone out of his way to make certain it had never happened. Odd, she thought. If she had fallen in love with someone like Ryder instead of Alberto, she would not be in this situation.

A burst of that unexpected warmth flooded her again as she sat in the dark cab of the truck, looking at the man behind the wheel. Despite his casual attitude and his protestations of a lack of interest in children, she had never forgotten the look on his face when he had held her baby in his hands.

And he had tried to save Maria, even knowing he had no chance against four armed men.

What would it be like to be in love with such a man? To have him love you in turn? Not an arrogant, unprincipled user like Alberto, but a man who, even if he was not happy about it, would help and not hurt?

He glanced at her then. "What is it with women and babies, anyway?" he asked, sounding almost exasperated.

"The continuation of the human race?" Ana said dryly, a bit stung by his tone.

He drew back slightly. And after a moment, she saw one corner of his mouth quirk. "Well, if you put it like that..."

Something about his reaction then made her say, almost shyly, "Thank you for trying to help Maria then, and for helping me now. It is good to know a man who will do the right thing."

For a moment he was very quiet. Then, softly, he said into the darkness, "Don't put your faith in me, Ana. I'll only let you down. It's what I'm best at."

"I don't believe that."

He laughed, a short, sharp, harsh sound. "Want a list of 'Ryder's-worse-than-useless' references? I can give you one. A very long one, with my brother, and probably my little sister, at the top. I'm the proverbial black sheep, in their book."

Ana could think of nothing to say to that. It seemed that, in his way, Ryder was as isolated from his family as she was from hers. He seemed to be saying he was the problem, not them. Yet she had no doubt that he was a good man, not anymore. She had had her doubts, even after the night of Maria's birth, but they had vanished by now.

"We're going to have to move fast," he said then, clearly changing the subject. "They're going to be right on my tail."

"We should have tied that man up as well," Ana said.

Ryder's mouth quirked again. "I didn't mean those guys."

It took her a moment to realize he meant the people he'd talked to on the phone.

"But…is that not a good thing?"

"Not for Maria."

Ana's breath caught. "What do you mean?"

"Their goal is to break this ring. To them, Maria's just another baby. If they get the job done in time to save her, fine, but that's not their focus."

She did not miss the subtext of that statement, that Maria was more than that to him. But this was not the time to dwell on that. She made herself concentrate on what he was saying.

"You mean that we must get the truth from this man, this doctor, quickly."

Ryder nodded. "I've suspected him for a while now, but

all I had was circumstantial. I could never find any solid evidence to tie him to the ring. And the feds, they're big on solid evidence. It doesn't do them any good to know who's guilty if they can't prove it."

"I do not care if they can prove it. All I want is my baby."

"I know."

"You think he is the leader of this baby-smuggling ring?"

"He's the most likely suspect I've come across."

"Then he will know where Maria has been taken. Who—" she stumbled over the horrible words "—has paid for her."

To her surprise, he reached out and took her hand, squeezed it. "We'll get her back, Ana. I swear we *will* get her back."

His hand felt warm, strong, comforting. Reassuring. And despite his warning not to put her faith in him, she found herself doing just that.

She hoped she would not regret it.

She prayed her daughter would not.

Chapter 16

Ryder had never had a wingman. He'd never needed one. Or so he'd thought. Now he seemed to have acquired one, albeit a wing-woman. And a beautiful, determined, and annoyingly smart one to boot.

He knew law enforcement people often worked with partners—even Furnell—and he'd always assumed it was for a very simple reason—two guns were better than one. But now he was beginning to understand the benefit of simply having someone else to bounce plans and ideas off.

And that's all it was. Nothing more than the benefit of having someone else there who called up odd feelings inside him. He didn't want to admit that because of Ana, he wondered what it would be like to have someone around all the time.

There was that forever thing again. He shoved it aside, but it was getting harder. He needed to focus, to concentrate. And he told himself to remember that Ana's determination to save her baby could well cloud what would normally be a razor-sharp thought process.

Again he wondered how she'd gotten herself into her situation.

"Where is Maria's father?" he asked bluntly. "Why isn't he helping you?"

For a moment she didn't answer, and he felt she might be too embarrassed, or simply deciding if he had the right to ask. When she did finally speak, it was an answer, but not exactly the one he'd been after.

"I would not accept his help."

"Why? You must have loved him."

He realized as soon as he said it that, on some level, he'd already known Ana Morales would never sleep with a man she didn't love. For some reason he didn't have time—or the desire—to stop and analyze why he was so edgy.

He thought he had heard emotion rising in her voice, and when she took a breath and went on, it burst through. "I hope he will soon be in prison, where he belongs."

Something knotted up hard deep in Ryder's gut. The anger, the scorn in her voice was unmistakable.

Well, now, he thought, there's a way to smash her trust in you. Just tell her you're doing this to get out of prison.

"Why?" he asked carefully. Then, as a horrible thought occurred to him, he slowed the car to look over at her. "Ana, he didn't rape you?"

She laughed, harshly. "He did not have to. He was my fiancé."

Ryder wasn't sure whether to be relieved or not. He put his eyes back on the road. "So you did love him."

"I loved who I thought he was. He was not that man." He heard an odd little sound in the darkness, realized she was taking in a deep breath, as if fighting back tears. He wished suddenly he'd never started this. "He is a criminal, brutal, wicked and immoral. And he is in league with a man who is even worse."

"Worse."

"My father," she said, and for the first time, despite all she'd been through, there was bitterness in her voice.

"I'm sorry," he said, feeling stupid for not having anything better to say.

"It killed my mother when she found out. I did not know this, until I learned the truth myself, but then it became clear." She let out a harsh, compressed breath. "Do you have any idea what it is like to despise your own father?"

The old pain jabbed him unexpectedly; he'd thought himself done with that long ago.

"Yes," he said flatly.

He heard her suck in a breath. She obviously hadn't expected his response.

"Not," he added, "that I ever knew him. I know who he is, know that my mother was one of many women all over the country. Know that he fathered a few of us he couldn't be bothered to acknowledge. Know that he's—"

He stopped suddenly, shocked at the realization that he'd been about to tell her who his father was. What was it about this woman that had his mind and mouth running in such crazy directions?

He hastened to rein it in, redirect, something. Anything. "But as far as I know he's just a sleazebag, not a criminal. Not that it would surprise me, of course, but since I never knew him, it doesn't bother me much. But your father..."

He let his voice trail off, hoping she would accept the rerouting of the conversation. Not just to get it off of something he didn't dare talk about—the famous Colton name—but because he genuinely wanted to know. Which put him even more on edge.

When she spoke at last, her voice was controlled, level and coolly dispassionate.

"My father is sophisticated, charming, polished and gracious. He is also arrogant, ruthless and utterly evil. He cares nothing for the law, or for justice, only for his own gains. He controls a network of underlings, who all do his bidding."

When she paused at last, he hazarded a guess. "One of them being your fiancé?"

"Alberto was more of an…associate," Ana said. A trace of emotion broke through once more as she gave a small, rueful laugh. "At least, that is how he was introduced to me. As a business partner. At the time, I still believed my father was an honorable businessman, who would only deal with other honorable men."

"Ana—"

"I was no more than a pawn to both of them. To my father, to secure what Alberto could offer him. To Alberto, to secure my father's benevolence."

"A bargaining chip," Ryder said.

Ana considered this, as if she'd never heard the phrase. Her English was so perfect—better than his, he admitted wryly—she had him thinking about the complexity of idioms, hardly a topic that ever would have occurred to him in his life before.

Before Ana, that is.

It startled him that he would even think that way, that even casually he would divide his life into a before and after marked by the simple event of meeting a woman.

"Yes," she said after a moment. "As in the days of royalty arranging marriages for their children to political advantage. And my father thought of himself as a kind of royalty."

"Sounds more like a mafia don," Ryder muttered.

"A...godfather, is it? Yes. That is very like what he is. Except that he has no rivals."

Something he realized he should have thought of before now hit Ryder. "How did you get away from him? From them?"

"I used my pregnancy. They are the kind of men who shy away from anything having to do with such things, anything truly female. When I went to see my physician, I went alone."

"They let you?"

He heard rather than saw her shrug. "They did not know yet that I knew the truth about their dealings. I had only just found out, and I hid it from them while I decided what I must do. Then when I found out I was pregnant, that decision was made for me. I could never bring my child into their world."

Strong was too weak a word for her.

"So you decided to leave not just your home, but your country?"

"My father's reach is long," she said. "So while Alberto was out bragging about his manhood, and my father was lighting candles to ensure a grandson, not an unwanted granddaughter, I pretended to be more ill than I was with morning sickness. They became used to my absence for hours at a time."

"You bought yourself a head start," Ryder said admiringly.

"When I had done all I could to prepare, I feigned a serious bout of illness on a night when my father was hosting a glittering party. I knew he wouldn't miss me for hours, probably not even think about me until morning. By then I was far away."

Ryder didn't want to think what a young, pregnant

woman must have gone through to get here. Despite her courage, she must have been frightened.

"Is Ana Morales your real name?"

"It is, in part. Morales was my mother's name. I will never again use my father's."

The irony of that bit deep; here they were, two fatherless souls, both using the names of mothers who had loved unwisely, thrown together in the midst of chaos. He had reluctantly gone along with Clay's change to *Colton* when the true identity of their father had been revealed, but he often reverted to *Grady* and was more comfortable with it.

"And," Ana added with emphasis, "I am in the process of doing things legally, to become a citizen. Jewel's family is powerful. They will help."

Speaking of the Coltons, Ryder thought wryly. But he pushed that aside for the moment.

"Maria," he began.

"She will never know," Ana said determinedly. "I will never tell her, about her father or her grandfather."

Ryder was grateful he had to pay attention to his driving for a moment, not because there was any traffic at this hour, but because they were nearing the turn they needed. It gave him a moment to ponder what Ana had said, and to wonder if he should tell her about a similar lie in his life.

And to wonder why he felt compelled to tell her every damn thing that popped into his head.

Finally, when he'd negotiated the turn and knew they only had a few more minutes to go, he spoke, the words he rarely said coming in a rush.

"For most of my life, I believed my father was an oil field worker, who died in an oil rig fire before my little sister was born."

Ana, as usual, did not miss his meaning. "But this was not true?"

"No. He was someone else entirely. Someone... wealthy, from a well-known family."

"Your mother must have had reason."

Ryder shrugged. "She did. We finally figured out that she was trying to protect us, that she knew he would never acknowledge us as his. He is..." He stopped the difficult flow of words, thinking there wasn't time now to list all the things Graham Colton was. And certainly not enough to list all the things he wasn't. "It doesn't matter. Point is, when we—my brother, sister and I—found out it was all a lie, that she'd died never telling us the truth, it was...hard."

It had been much more than that, of course. It had been stunning. So stunning that while Clay and Georgie had agreed to meet with the man who had fathered them, the man who had—for some reason Ryder had never trusted—finally reached out to them, Ryder hadn't wanted anything to do with him. And he was sure the father he'd never met would be happier that way. What Colton would want to acknowledge a reprobate like Ryder anyway? Even a slimeball like Graham Colton would think twice.

"You think I should tell her that both her father and grandfather are evil, terrible men?"

"I'm just saying that it was hard enough on us not knowing, and our father is just...pathologically self-centered," he said, using a phrase Boots had once used. "If your father and her father are as bad as you say, it could be worse for Maria. Maybe even dangerous."

Ana went still. "Dangerous?"

"I just mean that if it was me, and I had some connection to people like that, I'd want to know. So I could watch my back."

She said nothing for the rest of the drive, but Ryder could almost feel her thinking. He himself stayed quiet. He figured he'd talked more than enough. In fact, he'd talked about more things to this woman in the short time they'd known each other than to just about any woman he could remember that he wasn't related to.

Something about her—

He cut off his own thoughts when he realized they were nearing their destination. When he'd first suspected Breither was involved in the ring, he'd cased his home and office. He'd also located and checked out his old home, a vastly different place than the new, expansive, ostentatious residence he lived in now. Sitting regally alone on at least an acre of landscaped grounds, it was the kind of declaration of wealth that had always made Ryder think it would be easier to put up a sign saying "Hey, look, I'm rich!"

Envy, he'd told himself.

Recognizing a lack of class when he saw it, was what Boots had called it.

By then, he hadn't even seen anything odd in a convicted felon, sitting in a federal prison cell, discussing the finer points of class.

He parked near the edge of the property in the shadows of a tall pecan tree, something more common up in the hill country. For a moment he just studied the lay of the land.

He wondered what Ana thought of the place. If her father was as successful at his criminal undertakings as she'd said, she had likely grown up lacking nothing. Had she lived in a home like this one, or perhaps one even larger, more luxurious?

"Nice house," he murmured, not really wanting to open that door.

"Bought with the tears of mothers and babies," she said sharply.

"Yes," Ryder said simply.

She frowned, and after a moment said, "We must get inside, but how?"

He withheld any comment on her assumption that "we" would be going anywhere, and answered the last part. "When I was here before, I saw that there's a guesthouse and a pool with a pool house in the back, that would provide cover almost all the way up to the main house. It's only the last five yards or so that are exposed."

"But surely such a place will have alarms, perhaps dogs or armed guards?"

Armed guards?

With the realization that he had just gotten a glimpse into that prior life of hers he'd wondered about, Ryder said only, "No sign of dogs. Or guards. Alarmed, yes. But I can deal with that."

He was going to be glad he'd paid attention to his training that day, even if the thought had crossed his mind that being able to break into anywhere might come in very handy after he finished this job.

"What about others? Family?" She hesitated a split second, as if the idea that such a man would have children of his own was too much for her to conceive of. "Children?"

"Divorced. He lives here alone."

"Smart woman," Ana said sourly.

"I'm learning there's a lot to be said for smart women."

His own words startled Ryder; damn, the craziest stuff kept popping out.

"My father would disagree with you."

"His loss," Ryder said before forcing himself to turn his full attention to the task at hand. "Can you shoot?"

"If I must. My father had me instructed, for my own safety, he told me." Her tight smile was bitter. "Another of the many pieces I did not put together until too late, naive fool that I was."

"Not too late," Ryder told her. "You got out."

The smile she gave him then would stay with him forever, he thought. He handed her one of the liberated weapons. While she didn't look comfortable with it, she clearly wasn't afraid of it. She took a moment to look at it, while he pointed out the safety and told her how many rounds she had.

In the end, it was easier than he'd expected. Even though Ana insisted on going with him. She'd shown herself nervy enough and willing to let him take the lead. He was the one with the training, she'd said simply, so he hadn't had to waste time fighting her. They needed to move quickly; it was nearly dawn, a glance at his watch told him they had barely an hour of full darkness left, and what they had to do needed that cover.

As he'd told Ana, there were no dogs, no guards, but from his earlier surveillance, he noticed an up-to-date alarm system. An up-to-date alarm system that was, amazingly, not turned on. A red light flashed rhythmically, warning that the premises were unprotected.

So was Dr. Breither lazy, arrogant, stupid...or fiendishly clever? Had he gone off to bed so confident no one would dare mess with him that he hadn't bothered to set the system? Or was he just too stupid to remember?

Ana looked at him, and he saw the same questions in her eyes.

Not that it made any difference. No matter the reason, the answers they needed were inside this house, and there was no other way to get them except to go in.

At least the door was locked. Had it been open, every instinct Ryder had would have been screaming. But the combination of locked door but alarms not on left that final, most important question unanswered.

Had Breither been warned despite their precautions?

And was he smart enough to set a trap?

He pulled out the small leather case he called his break-in kit. It held a set of finely tempered lock picks, a tiny but powerful flashlight, and for situations that didn't require finesse, a glass cutter and a small suction cup.

A glance at the dead bolt told him it was a standard single cylinder, with a flip knob on the other side—cheap, for this expensive house, which said something, he was sure. He could probably pick it in a couple of minutes. But this back door that looked out on the pool area also had a large glass panel, and with the alarm off it only made sense to save that couple of minutes.

He placed the suction cup, cut around it in a circle large enough to allow his hand through, removed the glass, reached through to the dead bolt and flipped it open. He held back, waiting, watching, in case the apparently inactive alarm was instead an elaborate lure.

Nothing happened.

They stepped into the house, Ryder telling himself not to assume that their quarry was as stupid as this made him seem. He couldn't afford any mistaken assumptions.

Maria couldn't afford them.

Chapter 17

Ana had not known how she would feel when she faced this man Ryder suspected of being the leader of the baby-smuggling ring.

She felt utter contempt.

And disbelief. She was used to her father's urbane charm and air of strength and power. She had thought it would take at least that to put together this horrible endeavor. Was it truly possible that this skinny, cadaverous man with the beak nose, thinning hair and skittish eyes that refused to look straight at even inanimate objects, was the mastermind behind all this pain and heartbreak and anguish?

"But he is a cartoon," she exclaimed. "A caricature."

Ryder laughed. Ana liked the sound. An odd thought to have, under these conditions, but there it was.

It had taken him only a split second to get the locked door open through the hole he'd cut in the glass. They'd gone in quickly, but then Ryder made them both wait, something that went against the grain.

"Okay," he had finally whispered. "Not smart enough to set a trap."

She hadn't thought of that, that the disabled alarm system could have been a trap. She added cleverness and quick thinking to her growing list of things she admired about this man.

And upped her estimate of his courage and determination, since he had gone ahead anyway, even after thinking of the possibility.

Once inside, Ana had spared barely a glance at the furnishings of the house, thinking only that the entire place looked as if someone had hired a decorator and provided an unlimited budget for ostentation. Even her father had more taste; at least their home, luxurious though it was, appeared lived in.

The thought of the source of that unlimited budget had made her impatient. It also had her slipping Elena's knife into her hand once more; the gun Ryder had given her was at hand, but for a man like this she thought she might prefer the knife.

But now that she looked at him, a silly-looking, quivering man, cowering in the huge, ornate bed in a room that looked more like a high-end brothel, she felt only a pitying contempt.

"—it wasn't my idea," the man was saying his voice taking on a whine as his nervous eyes skipped from Ryder's weapon to hers.

"You're the last stop on this ugly railroad you've built. You're living—" Ryder gestured at the room "—on the proceeds."

"But I don't run it, I don't! I just needed the money, I—"

Ana lost patience. She stepped forward, leaning over the scrawny man as he held the covers with trembling hands, like some frightened virgin, as if they would protect him. Her knife glinted in the light from the overhead fixture Ryder had flipped on when they had first stepped in, startling the man into shocked stillness and giving them the edge.

Not that they'd needed it.

"You are unspeakably evil," Ana said. "You don't deserve to have ever lived, and certainly not to keep on doing so."

"Who are you?"

It came out as nearly a squeak, and Ryder laughed again. "She's who you should really be afraid of," he said. "You messed with the wrong mother, Breither. She'll carve you up like this silly bed if you don't talk. And she'll enjoy it, too."

Ana took an inward pleasure in Ryder's laughing threat, and in the way Breither's terrified eyes widened. "Mother…?" the man gulped out.

"I stand for all the mothers you have caused such pain and agony," she said, getting into the spirit of it. "Which is what I will deal to you in turn."

The man's already pale skin turned paler, and his muddy brown eyes suddenly rolled back in his head. He fell back onto the pile of pillows.

Ryder reached for him. "Damn," he said, but he was laughing. "He's out cold." He looked at Ana then. "You are amazing. And terrifying."

She reluctantly sheathed Elena's blade. "You do not seem terrified."

"I'm a man," Ryder said, his mouth quirking up at one corner in an expression she found oddly endearing, "not a mouse."

He certainly was that, she thought, and again the memory of his bare chest and flat belly flashed through her mind. She guessed that the rest of him was just as masculine, and wished she could some day find out for sure, a longing that startled her with its earthiness and power.

But he was definitely a different sort of man than she was used to in her life. He was strong, competent and clearly brave. Trustworthy? She thought so. He was doing the right thing, that was clear. But there was so much she didn't know. There were hidden depths to Ryder Grady that she did not understand, and she had no time to plumb them now.

That she wanted to unsettled her.

Her heart had betrayed her once, just as her mother's had betrayed her with her father. Yet she couldn't stop thinking that this, unlike her father and Alberto, was a real man. He was nothing like them, and that meant everything to a woman who had grown up under a very twisted vision of what a real man was.

Unlike this sham who had fainted at the mere sight of a woman with a weapon. Perhaps he knew he deserved to be separated from certain body parts.

"It is hard to believe he could be the person who organized this unspeakable thing," she said, voicing her earlier doubts.

"Yes." Ryder looked suddenly serious. "Yes, it's very hard to believe. It takes a certain amount of nerve to even consider an enterprise like this one. I don't think he has it."

She was gratified that he agreed with her, and so quickly. So she risked her second thought.

"But he knows who does."

Ryder nodded, something very like approval in his eyes. The expression warmed her unaccountably, and she felt a warmth rising in her cheeks that stunned her. She had sworn she would never hunger for a man's approval again, and yet here she was, basking in it. Was she becoming a fool yet again, and so quickly?

"We must find out," she said, her embarrassment at her own reaction sharpening her voice.

Ryder didn't take offense.

A real man, she thought again.

And this time no amount of internal chiding could dissuade her.

"That office down the hall," Ryder said, remembering glancing into the room as they searched for Breither.

She nodded. "I saw it."

"Put that blade to use on these fancy sheets."

She quickly did as he asked while he yanked the limp, unconscious man out of the bed and plopped him down into the wingback chair near the window. He took the strips of expensive fabric she handed him, twisted them into ropelike lengths and tied the man to the chair.

They were a good team, he thought as he tied off the last knot. He'd never been much of a team player, but this was different. This was the kind of thing he could get used to, more like having another part of yourself working in concert.

The old phrase, *My better half,* went through his mind, and his breath caught. He'd always thought that it was a joke used by housebroken men, but when he thought about Ana, there was no questioning that in any relationship, she would be the better half.

That he could see himself liking it that way, that he could imagine himself with her that way at all, rattled him so deeply he had to shake his head to clear it and get back to the matter at hand.

Moments later they were in the picture-perfect office.

"No computer," Ana said.

"Unless there's a laptop tucked away somewhere," Ryder said.

They began to search. They found no computer, but once Ryder had taken out his lockpicks and opened the heavy wood file cabinet against the wall, they found files upon files full of handwritten notes. Breither was apparently either old-fashioned, stuck in his ways, or too stupid to learn how to use a computer. Ryder's guess was it was some combination of all three.

"So much for the paperless revolution," Ryder muttered as he surveyed the files.

Ana didn't speak; she was flipping through the folder tabs quickly. "Nothing," she said, that edge still in her voice. If they found nothing and had to go back to Breither, Ryder didn't think much of the man's chances of holding out against her. He didn't have time to analyze why the thought made him smile inwardly.

"These are patient files," Ana said, closing the drawer, and adding grimly, "with an inordinate number marked with a sticker that says 'Deceased.'"

"Must be why he couldn't make any money as a doctor. His incompetence became known."

"Would he really keep papers to do with the babies in with all his old medical files?" she asked.

"This guy's squirrelly enough that I don't know what he'd do," Ryder said frankly.

But he kept searching, beginning with the bookcase behind a desk as heavily carved as the bed had been, while Ana kept going through files in another drawer of the filing cabinet.

"Maybe he's got a hidden compartment or something here," Ryder said. "These shelves aren't as deep as they could be."

Ana seemed to brighten at that thought and started helping him remove books from the shelves. Medical books, he noticed. Lots of them. How had someone who had done all the work to become a doctor become so perverted that he would go against every precept of the profession?

"'First do no harm,'" Ryder muttered.

Ana gave him a startled look. "Yes," she said, as if she'd been thinking exactly what he had. "That is what they swear. And yet he does this. It is abominable."

Ryder felt a small tug of satisfaction that they'd been on the same wavelength. But that didn't help the search. There was no trace of a hidden compartment. Ana was getting frustrated now. "We must find out. Do you think he is awake yet?"

Ryder stood there, holding the last book he'd removed from the shelves. Ironically, it was a four-inch-thick volume on obstetrics.

"If he's not, we'll wake him up," Ryder promised, dropping the book down on the pile they'd tossed haphazardly on the floor in their rush; Ryder had a certain respect for books, but no respect at all for anything belonging to this man.

Ana turned to go, then stopped when he didn't move in turn. He was looking at the book he'd just dropped, his mind racing.

"What?" she asked.

He shook his head. "I don't usually tackle books that big," he said, "but…"

He bent, reaching out to pick up the volume once more. "It's not as heavy as it should be," he said.

He opened the cover. Flipped the first few pages.

The only real pages there were.

Ana gasped when he turned the next leaf to expose a compartment hidden inside the book, where the pages had been hollowed out. The interior had been coated with something to make the sides of the space stiff, providing a perfectly sized place for the papers inside, more handwritten notes and what appeared to be records. Names, places, records of payments. Dozens of them.

Ana stared. "This many? They have stolen this many babies?"

Ryder glanced at her. Her expression was both horrified and furious. He guessed that to Ana, this was suddenly about more than just Maria. He knew her determination to save her little girl was boundless, but her face revealed a fury that would demand nothing less than the total destruction of this reprehensible operation, and the people who were perpetrating it.

God help them, he thought. Or not, he amended, as he scanned the papers from the compartment and saw page after page that represented tiny, helpless babies like Maria.

"Here," Ryder said, handing her some of the handwritten notes in what looked to him like some form of Spanish, but one he didn't recognize. "I speak better than I read. Take a look at these."

Ana took the papers and scanned them rapidly. "It is not you. It is *Nahuatl,*" she said.

"What?"

"It is the language of the Aztecs."

Ryder blinked. "Oh. Which means?"

"Nothing, perhaps. It might mean they were born or lived in Central Mexico, or their parents did."

"Anything else?"

"Some *Nahuatl* dialects are still spoken today, but mostly in rural areas. Some use it to show off their education, since it is among the most studied dialects in the Americas. It has existed since the seventh century."

He blinked again. "You sound like a teacher."

"It is what I hope to be. What I went to college to become."

College. Of course. Did you think her manner, her way of speaking, was learned on the streets of Mexico City?

Her father might be the Mexican equivalent of the Godfather, but Ana herself had called him sophisticated, charming and polished. Of course he would want his child to exhibit those same qualities, even if he did consider her more of a possession than a daughter.

So much for being on the same wavelength. She's way out of your league, Colton. Best remember that.

She turned her attention back to the pages. Her brow creased more deeply with each one, and her anger grew visibly.

"What?"

"They have taken at least some of the babies from poor parents, who signed them over. For a pittance, a tiny part of what you say they receive for the babies here."

"That figures."

She looked up at him. "This cannot make it legal, can it? You cannot sell your child!"

Ryder nearly took a step back in the face of her ferocity. "I'm no lawyer. I don't know about any of that."

She turned back to the papers, went through some more, and began to frown. "There is someone who is mentioned here. Several times. As if he were in charge of everything."

Ryder went still. "Who?"

"I don't know," Ana said, frustration tingeing her voice again. "He is not called by name. At least, not a real name. It is a sort of nickname, I think."

"What is it?"

"There is no literal translation to English that I know of. The closest I can say would be he is called 'Big.'"

"Is there any clue as to who or where he is?"

She held up a hand as she went back to the first note and

began to read again, more slowly. When she finally reached the last one, her frustration broke loose.

"There is nothing! No indication of who he is, where he is from, nothing."

"How do they talk about him? As if he were a stranger, a local, what?"

She got his meaning quickly. "They speak of him as if everyone already knows who he is."

"That's something, then," Ryder said, although he had no idea what.

"He must know more," Ana said determinedly. "And we must find out."

Ryder wasn't sure she was right about Breither's knowledge, but he agreed that they had to try. Back in the bedroom, they found the man revived and struggling to get free. When they stepped into the room he let out a little shriek; clearly he thought they'd gone.

Confronted with what they'd found, the man paled anew. Ana held the notes she'd translated in front of him. "Who is this man they speak of?"

"What?"

"This 'Big' they talk of in these notes. Who is he? Where is he?"

Breither gave her a look so blank Ryder knew it couldn't have been faked. "I don't know what you're talking about. I only know it was the authorization from the parents."

"Authorization?" Ana nearly spat it out.

"Most of the transactions were legitimate," Breither protested. "Those papers say so."

"Which explains why you're hiding them and burning the evidence," Ryder said. The man winced at the biting sarcasm in his voice.

"I never knew—"

"Do not dare to claim innocence," Ana warned him. She held the notes in front of him again. "Tell me who this 'Big' is."

"I tell you, I don't know. I can't read that stuff."

"Then why do you have it?" she said, resting her other hand pointedly on the knife in her pocket.

He whimpered. "They told me to keep it all, somewhere safe. To burn the envelopes they came in, so they couldn't be traced."

Ana pulled out the blade, held it with a familiarity and ease even Breither had to notice.

"They?" Ryder prompted.

Breither kept his terror-widened eyes on the knife. When Ana turned it so it gleamed in the light he suddenly couldn't talk fast enough.

"The papers would arrive, anonymously, in a post office box, when a package was in the system and due to arrive that night. That's all I know. I never saw or talked to anyone except the man who delivered the package."

Ryder believed him.

He also believed Ana was on the verge of committing mayhem. It was the "package in the system," as if the babies were something to be shipped like a pair of shoes, that had done it, he thought.

"I understand, but he's not worth it, *mija,*" he said softly. "He's just a cog in the wheel. And a sniveling coward at that. He just wet himself."

For a moment he didn't think she'd even heard him. But then she straightened, sheathing her ancestor's blade. She glanced at the dark stain forming on the expensive silk pajamas.

"The stench in here is foul," she said. "He does not deserve to live."

"Maybe he won't," Ryder said, injecting as much cheer as he could into his voice. "He doesn't strike me as the type who would have a lot of friends checking in on him when he doesn't show up for a couple of weeks."

The man whimpered again.

"I can no longer stand to be in the same room with him," Ana said and turned sharply. Ryder breathed again. He hadn't wanted to have to stop her, but he would have.

He was relieved that she'd backed off, he thought as he followed her out of the room. But he had no idea what she was going to do when she realized they were at a dead end.

When she realized that, barring a miracle, Maria was gone.

Chapter 18

"I am all right, truly," Ana said into the phone. "I will explain everything when I return."

"Your worthless fiancé didn't show up, did he?" Jewel asked, concern in her voice. She had been up for a couple of hours, even though it was just now six in the morning. Given her awful bouts with insomnia, Ana had guessed she would be awake, and therefore had risked the call.

Ana managed a creditable laugh at Jewel's question. "No. He considers himself well rid of us, I'm sure."

She doubted that. He was more likely furious with embarrassment at having his fiancée flee from him in the middle of the night. While her father was likely just furious, as he would be at one of his dogs who dared to disobey him. She didn't think he would have her put down, as he had one dog who had particularly displeased him, but sometimes she wasn't so certain of that. Especially since the dog had been her own favorite, and his misdeed had been to hesitate before leaving Ana's side when her father had called him.

"Is there any news of the baby smugglers?" Ana asked, trying to keep her tone casual.

"No developments. Adam was here early this morning, and he mentioned that they're getting very frustrated at the lack of progress."

Ana's heart sank. Not that she had expected anything different, but she had harbored a tiny hope that something might have changed.

The real purpose of her early-morning call was now accomplished, but she knew she needed to mask it with more normal chatter. She turned to the one most likely to distract Jewel—the besotted deputy, obviously checking on her in the early hours.

"And is there any progress on that front?" she asked, using the almost teasing tone she usually adopted when asking Jewel about the handsome Adam Rawlings, so clearly enthralled with her.

"Not as far as he's concerned," Jewel said. "He still wants more than I'm ready to give."

At the serious answer, Ana's voice became serious as well. "Then you are being wise."

Jewel laughed. "You're the only one who thinks so. Everybody else seems to think I should go for it."

"They only wish you to be happy. But no one knows what will do that better than you yourself."

"Ah, you are a wise one, my friend."

If so, it came much too late, Ana thought as she ended the call a few moments later.

"Nothing?" Ryder asked after a moment.

"Nothing," she confirmed. "You are not surprised."

Ryder shrugged as he drove. "The sheriff has a lot of other things on his plate just now. This is the only thing on mine."

She liked the single-minded sound of that, although so far even their combined determination had not accomplished the goal.

For the first time, she looked around, realized she did not recognize anything. "Where are we going?"

He seemed to hesitate for a moment before answering. "Back to my motel."

"Fine," she said. She wanted a quiet place to go through the notes again, where she could concentrate and perhaps find something she had missed in her rapid mental translation.

She heard him chuckle. It sounded rueful, and a glance at him showed a matching expression on his face. "I'm guessing," he said, "that does not have the same connotations in your world."

"I am not ignorant," she said, rather stiffly. "I presumed you did not mean it in that way."

His expression changed. "I'm not sure whether to be flattered or insulted," he said with a wry quirk to his mouth.

"I am sure there is a woman in your life who would take offense for you," she said. "Or at you, were you to pursue such a path."

To her chagrin, he laughed. "I love the way you talk when you're angry."

When she was angry, she knew her speech became more formal, especially in English. Although it was the language she knew best after her own, it was still not her first language. She tended to be extra careful when her emotions were roiled, to be certain she did not make any mistakes.

But that did not mean she appreciated being laughed at.

"I'm sorry," Ryder said. "I'm sure you're in no mood for jokes."

Having taken the wind right out of her anger—although she was fairly certain she had mangled that idiom—he was looking at her contritely.

"No," she agreed. "I cannot seem to find my sense of humor."

"It will come back with Maria," he said.

She gave him a grateful smile for that. He smiled back, and she thought it lovely, despite the fact that his face was still slightly swollen. It reminded her that this man had fought for Maria, was still fighting for her, going on when she was certain he would like nothing more than to lie down and rest what had to be an aching body.

A real man, she thought yet again.

"Ana?"

"Yes?"

He didn't look at her when he said quietly, "There isn't a woman to take offense."

"Oh."

She wondered why he'd felt it necessary to explain that.

She wondered why she felt so gratified that he had.

She gave herself a mental shake; there was no time for such thoughts. She turned to look forward through the windshield again, to the east and the rising sun. The dawn of the first day without her baby in her arms.

She vowed it would also be the last.

Ryder was more than grateful for the plentiful hot water supply at the motel. He let it pour over his aching body. It seemed like a lifetime ago rather than just yesterday that he had stood here last. It had been routine, that last shower, not a matter of gingerly dodging the scrapes, sore spots, and developing bruises.

When he dried off and checked his chest and back in the

mirror, the wounds weren't as bad as he'd expected. There were going to be bruises all right, lots of them, but as he poked and prodded and took experimental deep breaths, he decided at the worst a rib or two might be cracked.

His face, on the other hand, was a lost cause. The left side was still swollen, and he had the beginnings of a brutal shiner to go with his split lip.

Looking like this, he'd have a hard time picking up a woman even in the worst roadhouse dive.

His lack of interest in every woman except for the one in the next room made him wince.

With a smothered sigh he turned away from the mirror. The last time he'd looked this bad was after he and Jorge Vega had crashed that motorcycle they'd taken for a joyride when he was thirteen. That had been the beginning of the end for Clay.

He felt a pang of sympathy for what he'd put his brother through; it couldn't have been easy to try and keep their little family together when he'd only been eighteen himself. But Clay had done it. Ryder began to think about the enormity of that task. Clay had had to fight some government agency that didn't think he was capable of handling a fourteen-year-old sister and a sixteen-year-old hellion of a brother. What kind of hard sell had his brother had to do to keep them all together?

And what good had it done? One ends up pregnant and dumped, the other in prison?

For one of the few times in his life, Ryder actually felt a pang of guilt. Clay had tried, more than most brothers would have, but Ryder hadn't listened. He'd developed the knack of tuning out his brother as he'd tuned out teachers at school, letting his mind wander to the next bit of fun on the horizon.

He pulled on his last clean pair of jeans, thinking he'd have to take Mrs. Sanchez up on her offer of laundry services, and grabbed the T-shirt he'd brought in with him. Pulling it on made him wince, but he didn't want Ana seeing his chest and back now that the bruises were rising to the surface.

He also didn't want to be half naked in the same room with her. The last time he'd been hurting too much. Now, he was hurting a little less…

Barefoot, he opened the door into the main room. When he'd gone in for his shower, she had been seated at the small table by the one window, the notes they'd found spread out before her. But although the papers were still there, she was not.

A tiny sound alerted him, and he stepped into the room and looked in that direction.

She was curled up on the bed in a tight little ball, her body shaking, and he realized that she was crying.

Ryder felt as if Mr. E had just delivered a knockout punch. He couldn't take this. Without faltering, she'd gone through a night of childbirth that would have left many men paralyzed.

"Ana," he whispered, sitting down on the bed beside her.

"I can find nothing," she gulped out between sobs. "There is all this talk in the notes about this person 'Big,' but there is nothing to tell us who or where he is. Nothing."

He reached out, unable to stop himself from touching her.

"Don't cry," he said, knowing even as he uttered the words how ridiculously inadequate they were. Why shouldn't she cry?

She lifted her head to look at him. Her eyes were reddened, her cheeks wet, and she was still beautiful.

"My baby," she choked out. "My baby."

Ryder saw with a sinking heart that it had hit her. That

she had realized they were at a dead end, that they had no leads, no clues, nothing.

Driven by a need to comfort unlike anything he'd ever felt for a woman before, he lay down beside her and pulled her into his arms.

"We're not giving up, Ana," he whispered against her hair. "We're not giving up."

She shuddered, sobs taking her once again. He wished he had even the slightest idea how he was going to keep the promise he'd made to this woman, and to a tiny little girl who was likely already lost to them.

He held her as she wept, and she let him. That alone was a bit of a wonder, he thought. Ana Morales was strong and fierce and tough when she had to be, and even as big an idiot as he was when it came to women couldn't miss the trust that implied.

Gradually she uncurled from her self-protective ball, and he could feel the soft, warm length of her pressed against him. If she'd been anyone else, if the circumstances had been any different, he would have made a move. He would like nothing more than to make love to this woman. He was good enough to make her forget her anguish, for a few moments at least, and perhaps allow her the peace of sleep for a few hours.

Again he told himself his self-control came because it was physically wrong for her that he wanted to make love rather than simply having sex. Also, the timing was wrong. Pressuring her at a time like this, with her full being focused on her daughter, would be one of the biggest mistakes of his life.

His worry about timing now—anytime had been the right time—was just another item on the growing list of things that were different with Ana.

But the reasons for it, whatever and however many there were, didn't change the fact that it was the hardest damn thing he'd ever done.

"We're not giving up, Ana," he said for a third time. And as she wept he held her, forcing himself to think, not of how good she felt in his arms, of how much he wished things were different and he could indulge the need that was threatening to rage out of control, but of what the hell to do next.

Chapter 19

When she had awakened in his arms, Ana had been amazed, then embarrassed that she had slept. She was not sure he had, since he had been awake and looking at her when she had opened her eyes. The smile he had given her then, even lopsided thanks to his obviously still tender lip, had warmed her in the instant before reality had flooded back. She felt guilty for sleeping while her baby was missing.

"You needed to rest," he'd said, accurately assessing her reaction. "And now we get back to it."

She had not been at all sure what there was to get back to, but she'd been encouraged that he apparently had some sort of plan, so she had hastened to quickly shower while he went out to find coffee. As she had showered, she had become aware of the aching fullness of breasts used to nursing Maria every few hours.

She dug through the pink bag and brought out the manual

breast pump that was in a side pocket. She had thanked Macy Ward—Yates now, she corrected herself—who had given it to her, but had also said she had no intention of being separated from her baby long enough to need it. Macy, who said she'd only gotten her sense of humor back since Fisher Yates had changed her life, had laughed and told her not to tempt fate with that kind of challenge.

She sent the tall brunette a silent apology for doubting her.

And chastised herself for tempting that fate to prove her wrong. Tears began anew as she went about the business of expressing the milk her baby should be having right now, and fierce worry at how Maria was being treated welled up inside her.

She had just finished when the door opened. She swiftly adjusted her bra and pulled her sweater down before Ryder stepped into the room. He stopped just after closing the door, two steaming cups in his hand, looking at the device in her hand curiously. She explained, expecting him to become embarrassed at the very thought. As she was embarrassed by the thought that if he had been thirty seconds earlier, he would have walked in on her with her breasts bared.

But Ryder just looked at her, an odd, almost wistful expression on his face. A distant, unfocused sort of look, as if he were picturing something else.

Then, suddenly, he was back, holding out one of the steaming cups to her.

"We're not giving up," he said yet again.

"I know," she said, eyeing the cup doubtfully.

"I got you hot chocolate," he said. "The lady said that was better than coffee for you."

Ana stared at him as she took the chocolate. Had the rakish, wild—and slightly battered-looking—Ryder actually asked some woman at a coffee shop what would be safe for a nursing mother to drink? Somehow that touched her as much as anything else he had done, and the tears threatened again.

She fought them down as she took the first sip, surprised at how good it felt, even knowing how hot it likely was outside.

While she drank, she watched Ryder gather up what appeared to be all his meager belongings. Or at least, all he had here in this motel room; she realized with a little shock that she did not even know where he really lived. She had trusted this man with the most important task of her life, and she did not even know if he lived in a house, an apartment, or a tiny room like this one in some other town.

"You are packing?" she asked as he stuffed things into a large canvas backpack.

"Don't know when, or if, I'll be back here. And some of it might come in handy."

She brightened at the implications of that. "You have a plan?"

He grimaced. "Nothing so organized. Just the only thing I can think of to do."

"Which is?"

"Shotgun," he said.

Ana blinked, wondering if this meant something other than the weapon it seemed to refer to, if it were some American English slang term she'd somehow missed.

"You fire a shotgun," he said, "the pellets spread out in all directions. You fire often enough, sometimes you get lucky and hit the right thing."

She soon understood what he meant, literally. The next few hours were a whirlwind of action, Ryder tracking down every person he thought might have a connection to the baby ring. Ana noticed he took a different tack with different people, angry and intimidating with some, persuasive with others, going from sharp and frighteningly forceful to gently coaxing. Shaking them down, he called it. But so far the results had been negligible.

When they confronted some of the clients of the ring, couples so desperate for a baby they had asked no questions, even Ana felt the stirrings of an unwelcome sympathy.

Ryder had told her her job with those people was to represent Maria. To show them the truth of what they had done in their vehement insistence on getting a baby. That she could do easily enough.

As they proceeded, she had the thought that they worked well together. It was unexpected, as so much had been with this man, but undeniable as well. And she could not seem to stop herself from wondering what it would be like to have this man in her life, the kind of man who would not see her as a possession but a partner, who would be proud rather than annoyed at her intelligence, and who understood her determination to raise her baby in a better place.

She told herself her yearnings, her imaginings of a long, golden future with Ryder were just that, pure imagination.

It was hard to accept when the solid, strong reality of the man was right before her.

He left the number of Ana's cell phone with each person they confronted. "You are hoping that they will have second thoughts or remember something after we leave? That they will call?" she asked when they'd made yet another stop. They were on the outskirts of San Antonio now, in a quiet residential neighborhood that seemed too peaceful and picturesque to harbor such evil doings.

"Or someone will," Ryder said, almost absently as he negotiated the ramp onto Interstate-35.

Someone? Ana wondered. It took her a moment to

realize he meant someone from the ring itself. That he thought one of the people they'd talked to—shaken down—would report to his bosses what had happened, that the man they had left for dead was not, and was now openly after them.

With his bruised face always before her, the risk Ryder was taking was never out of her mind. Yet she suddenly realized the danger he was putting himself in, that he was in fact asking for.

And yet he kept going. It was impossible to remain distraught in the face of Ryder's tireless pursuit.

And unaccountably, despite the fact that nothing they'd done so far had seemed to get them any closer to finding Maria, her spirits rose.

He was getting toward the end of his list of people to arm-twist, badger, and if necessary bite, Ryder thought. And so far he'd accomplished nothing but to advertise himself, not just blowing his cover but incinerating it and putting up a billboard to mark the spot.

Getting Maria back was the priority now. The baby ring was secondary.

Which meant he'd likely signed and sealed the orders that would send him back to prison himself.

"What was the deal you made?"

Ryder nearly choked on his own breath. He shot her a sideways look. "What are you, a mind reader?"

She lowered her gaze. "I am sorry. I should not have asked. You are helping me, helping Maria, that should be enough."

He fought the urge to reach out and take her hand. He hadn't meant to snap, she'd just startled him, so close was her question to what had just gone through his mind.

The idea that simply touching her hand, holding it, seemed like the thing he wanted most unsettled him anew. What the hell was happening to him? How had he gotten to the point where a mere look, a brush of skin, was enough, when it was from this woman? And why couldn't he seem to find the fortitude to back the hell off?

Maybe you can't, but I'll bet she can, he told himself.

"The deal I made," he said, his voice flat, "was to get out of prison. Happy now?"

If she was shocked, it didn't show. "Why were you in prison?"

She was so calm he would have thought she hadn't heard him right if she hadn't repeated the word back to him.

"It was the culmination of a misspent life," he said.

"In America, are not charges usually more…specific?"

What was with this woman? Why wasn't she cringing away from him instead of discussing this as if it were the weather?

"It doesn't matter. I didn't do what they put me in for—at least, not knowingly—but I've done enough to end up there anyway."

"Tell me," she said.

Right, he thought.

But he did. Somehow, in his efforts to avoid it, he ended up spilling it all, things he'd never talked about with anyone except Boots. Like some lovesick kid, he poured out his entire pitiful history to her. And she listened. Not that she had much choice, stuck here in the truck's cab with him, but she could have told him to shut up. And when he finally finished, he fervently wished that she had.

He waited, certain she sadly regretted that "Tell me," now. His life no doubt seemed a cakewalk compared to what she'd been through, and she probably thought him a whiner. He wasn't sure she wasn't right. He—

"Odd, is it not? That while my family was large and close, they were of no more good to me than yours to you."

Of all the things she could have said, nothing could have startled him more. "You mean I was no good to them."

"No. They obviously did not understand what you needed, just as mine did not understand—or care about—my needs."

"My brother tried," Ryder said, stirred to an uncharacteristic defense. "We just…always fought."

"I have two older brothers. They are very close. I believe they would die for each other. But they care little for the rest of the family."

"I guess we were just too different, my brother and I," Ryder said, wondering where that piece of understanding had floated up from. "We could barely stand each other. Maybe even hated each other."

She shook her head. "I doubt it is truly that way." When she went on, her tone was different, almost speculative. "The man who owns the ranch, Jewel's friend Clay, he also had a brother he always fought with. But when he learned that brother had died, he was devastated, as any brother would be. He is still fiercely grieving."

Ryder went ice cold. The oddity of suppressing a shiver in the August heat didn't even register.

"Died? Clay thinks…his brother died?"

"Yes. Seven months ago. Jewel told me."

When he got out for this assignment. That must be part of the cover. A part they hadn't told him about.

But he hadn't told anyone, except Boots, that he even had a brother. No one at the prison knew, nor did his new employers.

"How did he find out?" He couldn't help the hoarseness

of his voice, but Ana answered as if he'd asked a simple, normal question.

"He wrote to his brother, to try and make amends. It came back. He wrote again. The same thing happened. He called, and was given—Jewel called it the runaround?—so he went to see him in person."

Ryder swallowed tightly. "He went…to see him?"

"That is when he was told. He is still grieving deeply, and cannot forgive himself for waiting too long."

Ryder swallowed tightly. Emotions too deep and old to name swirled around inside him. But finally, belatedly, something occurred to him; there had been a very pointed note in Ana's voice as she'd told him this story. And then there were the details. More than seemed natural for the situation from her point of view.

So maybe you're wrong about her point of view, he thought. He looked at her, steadily, and at last she gave him what he'd suspected.

"He cannot forgive himself for giving up on his brother." She held his gaze. "For giving up on you."

Ryder let out the breath he hadn't even been aware of holding. "How did you know?"

"I was not sure, until now, when you said you and your brother might even hate each other. Jewel told me that was Clay's greatest regret, that his brother had…died thinking he hated him."

Ryder tried to wrap his mind around that. He could see Clay feeling responsible for the breach—after all, his brother felt responsible for damn near everything—but the image of a grieving, saddened Clay, over him of all people, was more than he could conjure up.

"Your brother is, by all I have heard, a good man."

"He always was. It was me who was the problem. I—"

The ring of her cell phone cut off his words and short-circuited the turmoil in his gut. He held his breath again as she picked up the phone and looked at the caller ID.

"It is not Jewel," she said, and he saw a tremor go through her. "It is a restricted number."

Had all his shaking yielded some fruit after all? Ryder took the phone and flipped it open.

"Talk," he said shortly.

"Back off." The voice was male, but so muffled, either by something over the mouthpiece or by electronic means, he couldn't tell anything more.

"Can't do that."

"You'll regret it."

"Probably," Ryder agreed. "But I want her back. Now."

The caller didn't pretend to misunderstand. "The baby?" The voice laughed then, giving Ryder a moment to focus on his way of speaking; he thought there was a trace of an accent, but as muffled as it was he couldn't be sure. "I grant you, her mother's a pretty hot piece of ass. But is she worth dying for?"

Initially, Ryder bridled at that description of Ana, even though, had he seen her for the first time without all the entanglement, he might have thought pretty much the same thing. She was, after all, incredibly attractive. He had the memory of long, aching hours of holding her and holding back to prove that.

But that reaction was blasted away by the realization that the question the voice had asked had provoked. Time was, he would have laughingly answered that there was nothing in this world he counted worth dying for. His life might not be worth much, but he still wouldn't give it up for something as stupid as a cause.

Or for someone else.

But now he wasn't so sure.

"Have to think about it, *cabrón?* Then I'll make you a deal. A trade. The baby…for you."

The voice laughed again as Ryder's mind raced. Was this Mr. E, looking for payback for that kneecap? Or was it Alcazar himself, demanding retribution for Ryder daring to infiltrate his operation?

"I'll call you back with details," the voice said, and the phone went dead.

It didn't matter who it was, Ryder told himself. What mattered was making sure whoever it was kept his end of the deal.

And it wasn't until that went through his mind that he realized he had every intention of making this devil's bargain. If it would put Maria back in her mother's arms, he would do a lot worse.

Besides, he'd escaped from them once. He could do it again. And even if it took some time, he'd survived prison, hadn't he? He could hold on long enough.

"What is it?" Ana asked, her voice shaking. "Was it the men who have Maria?"

"Yes."

She stifled a cry.

"It's all right," Ryder said, knowing he couldn't tell her the truth, it would only add to her burden. "We're starting negotiations."

"Negotiations?"

"We'll get her back, Ana. We *will* get her back. I promise you."

He hoped he wasn't telling the biggest lie of his misbegotten life.

Chapter 20

"Italy?"

Ana stared at the screen of the self-service check-in kiosk. The bustle of the San Antonio airport was simply background noise to her now, the people all around vaguely resented for not having such horror in their lives.

"So it seems," Ryder muttered.

Ana looked at him for a long, silent moment. When they'd parked the truck, he had stowed the weapons behind the seat with obvious regret. But he clearly knew there was no way he could get a weapon through security.

"They have taken my baby to Italy?" she asked, bewildered.

"Ana," Ryder said, "I don't know what they're doing. Maybe you should stay here, in case this is a false lead."

He had been trying to get her to agree to stay behind since the mysterious voice had called again, with the numbers for two e-tickets and instructions to be at the airport within the hour, and to board the plane without drawing any attention.

"But he said for both of us to take this flight. And if he has Maria, I must be there."

"If he does, I'll bring her back, Ana."

"I know you would," she said, believing it with a faith she was surprised to find was so strong. "But she is my daughter, and my responsibility."

"What if this is just a trick, to get us out of their way?"

As he voiced her worst fear, that while they were in Italy Maria would disappear irrevocably, Ana felt a shiver of pure terror grip her. It was a moment before she could control it and ask, "Do you believe that it is?"

Ryder shifted uncomfortably, and she read the answer in his eyes before he spoke. "No."

"Then we go to Venice."

Ana was thankful he did not argue with her. Perhaps it was because they did not have much time; they had to find the rental locker the mysterious voice had directed them to and still make it to the gate.

"Anna Giovanni," Ana read as he handed her a very real-looking Italian passport. "And you are?"

"Antonio Giovanni," he said. "Not too original. But I don't much like that they were able to find a photograph of you."

Ana shrugged; it was indeed a photo of her, not just someone who resembled her. "But it is from school, my graduation," she said. "It would not be hard to find, even to get from the university website."

"But they know who you are."

"They do now, yes. But that is not surprising, is it, after what we have done these last two days?"

"Maybe," Ryder said, but he didn't sound convinced.

"What of you? Your photograph?"

"That is a mug shot," Ryder said with a grimace. "Also public record. They just cropped it a little."

It was not until they were at their gate that Ana said, more than a little worriedly, "To do this so quickly…they are very efficient."

"Yes," Ryder agreed, and she did not think she'd mistaken the grim note in his voice.

"Benvenuto," the flight attendant said cheerfully as they boarded.

"Grazie." Ana thanked him for the welcome, automatically in Italian, earning her a sideways look from Ryder.

"Italian, too?"

"And French," she said. "And I can manage a bit of Greek, and a bit less German."

"Handy," he muttered, and she wondered why he didn't sound very happy about it.

She had many hours to think on the long flight. She tried to rest, telling herself she would need to be alert and ready when they landed. But she could only doze, never really sleeping, going just deep enough for awful imaginings about Maria's fate to shock her awake. It was only when Ryder put his arm around her after a particularly nasty one that she was finally able to relax.

When she woke that time, it was a gentler thing, and she found herself sleepily snuggling against his warmth. He was awake, and she wondered if he'd gotten any rest himself; he had to be as tired as she was, and must feel even worse, still aching from the beating he'd taken.

"Tell me about your family," she said impulsively.

"I don't have—"

He stopped suddenly, as if only now remembering that she knew who he really was. Would he refuse? She had poured out her sordid story, admitted to him the truth of her father and her fiancé. She knew this did not mean he had to do the same in return, knew that often men did not have the same view of sharing, bonding through the telling of secrets that many women had.

But still, these were hardly ordinary circumstances, she thought.

Just when she thought he indeed was not going to answer, he started to talk. It was clear from the awkwardness of it that he had not done this often, and she knew she would need to take care that he not regret it later.

That she was even thinking of later, and that they would still be together, was something she couldn't deal with just now. So she quietly listened to his halting tale of a free-spirited, fiery-haired rodeo rider who had fallen hard for the worst possible man for her, and ended up with three children whose father had never even acknowledged their existence until long after her too-early death.

"I think she worked herself to death," Ryder said, and Ana couldn't blame him for the bitter note in his voice.

She wondered if that was why he had shied away from settling down to a normal occupation, or if it was simply that he had inherited his mother's free spirit and couldn't handle settling down at all.

"Your father," she said, remembering what Jewel had explained when she'd first come to Hopechest Ranch, "he is related to the famous Colton, the man running for your presidency?"

"The black sheep brother," Ryder said sourly. "That would be dear ol' dad."

Ana hesitated before saying carefully, "You have called yourself this name as well, the black sheep. Do you see yourself as like your father?"

"No!"

The answer was so vehement that Ana had to hide a smile.

"Good. Because you are nothing like him."

He blinked, as if startled by her certainty. "How do you know?"

"A man who would go halfway around the world to help a baby who is not even his, would hardly abandon one of his own."

He stared at her for a long silent moment. "But I feel as if she's...partly mine."

"She is," Ana said quietly, admitting for the first time that some part of her daughter—and some part of herself—would always belong to this man who had come in out of the darkness to help them when they were most in need.

Ryder looked away then, quickly, as if he were embarrassed by the admission. Ana felt a flood of tenderness, and wished things were different so that she could show him how she felt. She had known that he wanted her, it had been impossible to miss his state of arousal when he had held her so gently for those agonizing hours in his motel room. That he hadn't even tried to act upon it told her many things, not the least of which was that he cared.

Had her body been healed already, would she have acquiesced? She did not know. She did not want to believe she would have fallen into bed with a man she barely knew, but she suspected it might have been a harder battle than she would like to admit.

Perhaps she was just destined to always fall in love with the wrong man, she thought.

Love?

Not, she told herself. Surely not.

She realized slowly that she was still leaning into him, loath to relinquish the closeness that had allowed her to rest.

Maybe not.

She stole a quick, sideways glance at Ryder. He was to her right, so she got the full impact of the beating he'd taken for Maria.

Maybe.

But she had no right to even consider such things until Maria was safe. Ana forced such thoughts out of her mind.

But she didn't move away from Ryder's warmth.

For a guy who'd never been farther away from the United States than Saltillo, Mexico, this should have been an exciting trip. Could have been, if you added in the beautiful, fascinating, incredibly courageous woman at his side.

He liked the sound of that "at his side" stuff. But it was the courageous part that threw cold water on the expedition. Much as he might—to his own bemusement—like the idea of a long, romantic trip with Ana Morales, the circumstances were what they were. They had a long way to go before he could let his thoughts turn to romance.

But he was willing to wait. That alone told him how much he'd come to feel for her.

Of course, he had to survive this first.

The mundaneness of being met by a driver holding a card with the names on their false ID nearly made him laugh. But that ordinariness was soon forgotten as, a few minutes later, the same driver ushered them from the car to a waiting boat, for which he was also apparently the wheelman. Ryder barely had time to glance around, marveling at this postcard image of buildings and canals, with the oddly shaped gondolas bobbing gently.

This boat was a racy-looking powerboat, however, and he had the thought that big houses in Texas weren't the only thing this smuggling ring had paid for.

It went so much against his nature to allow the driver to wrap a black cloth around his head as a blindfold that it took everything he had to sit still. His vision cut off, he heard the rustle of cloth as the man apparently did the same thing to Ana.

The boat began to move—surprisingly slowly and quietly, Ryder thought, until it occurred to him that perhaps there were laws here about speed and noise. The last thing these people would want was to attract attention. Not that that explained the fancy boat itself, but—

He heard Ana make a quiet, quivering sound that she was obviously trying to stifle. Instinctively he put an arm around her. She leaned into him, much as she had on the plane.

Despite everything, including the uncertainty of his own life span just now, he liked it just as much. Wanted nothing more than to have an endless string of such moments with her, forever.

And that he'd just thought once more of the word *forever* in conjunction with a woman came as only a minor shock this time.

They made several turns, and Ryder began to learn the pattern, the change in the sound of the water against the hull, the barely perceptible lean as the boat changed direction. He started out noting what directions they were traveling in and for how far, thinking about finding the place again. But when he realized that if he followed his mental map they would have gone in a big circle twice, he gave up.

Finally the boat slowed, and he heard the lap of water against stone much closer this time. Their driver called out, although in Italian. At least Ryder assumed it was Italian. Someone ashore answered.

"He wants them to tie up the boat," Ana whispered.

He tightened his arm around her in thanks; even now her quick mind never faltered.

Getting off the boat blindfolded was tricky, and his hands clenched into fists when he heard Ana say something sharply to one of the men, something that sounded like "*diavolo.*" He could guess at the satanic reference, but didn't want to know what the man had done to earn it; he was having enough trouble allowing himself to be trundled along like so much baggage.

Like a duffel bag, he thought, and anger spiked through him, reminding him of exactly why they were here, because these people had thought of Maria, and dozens like her, as nothing more than baggage.

There was the sound and feel of stone beneath their feet as the two men now herded them along. Ryder could tell when they stepped inside a building by the change in the sound of their steps, by the echo of movement, by the very feel of the air around them. They kept going and the sounds changed again, echoed louder, as if they were walking down a hallway.

They turned to the left, and Ryder heard the sound of a door opening. Their escorts pushed them forward, he assumed into a room. He heard the door close behind them, and realized he didn't know if their two shepherds had come into the room with them or not.

A baby cried.

"Maria!" Ana's shout was joyous, but Ryder heard a thickness to it, wondered if she, too, was crying.

Ryder couldn't hear or sense the two men, so decided to risk yanking off the blindfold. He found Ana had already done the same, although he could barely see her in the darkened room. She threw down the cloth and started toward the crying baby; Ryder grabbed her and held her back.

"Wait, Ana. It could be a trap."

"But it is Maria! I know my baby's voice."

"I'm not saying it's not, just—"

A loud peel of laughter echoed off the walls, filling the room eerily.

"Have you not learned there's no logic in women?"

Ryder went still; it was the voice from the phone. The muffled effect must have been electronic, because it was the same here, coming over what had to be a speaker somewhere at the far end of the room.

"But I must thank you, Ana, for keeping your end of the bargain. I have been looking for this man."

"What does he mean? What bargain?" Ana asked.

"It doesn't matter," Ryder whispered to her. "Just don't agree to anything until you have Maria in your arms."

"No one crosses me and lives to speak of it," the voice said. "It simply isn't good for business."

"Ryder—" Ana began, but the distorted voice cut her off.

"There is a rope on the wall behind you, Ana. Get it, and tie his hands behind him."

"What?"

Ana sounded bewildered, but Ryder knew her well enough by now to guess that her mind was racing.

"It's all right," he said to her, almost absently as he surreptitiously fiddled with the belt at his waist. "Do what he says."

"But you—"

"If you want Maria back, do what he says."

There was a split-second's pause before he heard her breathe a low, reverent oath. "This is the bargain? You, for my baby?"

The voice laughed again. "You did not tell her that was the deal—your life for the baby's life? How noble of you.

How self-sacrificing." The laugh again, this time it sounded utterly gleeful. "How delicious."

"Do it, Ana," Ryder told her.

"I cannot," Ana said, urgently. "He will kill you, and I…cannot bear that."

The simple emotion in her voice made Ryder's chest tighten. Wouldn't it just figure that he would finally find the woman who made him want to mend his ways only to get himself killed before he'd so much as kissed her?

"Do it, Ana. For Maria. It will be all right."

He wished he was more certain of that himself. He'd never thought much about dying; he didn't guess people did at the ripe old age of twenty-four. Oh, there had always been the chance one of his risky escapades could have gotten him killed, but he'd always figured he didn't care.

And now that he did, now that, amazingly, for the first time in his life he was thinking about the future, a real future, here he was, likely going to die sooner rather than later.

And painfully rather than peacefully.

But at least it would be for a reason. A good reason, he told himself as the baby cried again. That was more than he would have likely gotten had he continued down his scapegrace path.

"Do it now," ordered the voice, "or I will quiet this baby permanently."

Ryder heard Ana stifle a tiny cry. "Do it, Ana," he told her again, still working at slipping his belt through the loops on his jeans.

She moved then, following orders she clearly did not want to obey. She tied his hands, loosely, then at the voice's order, retied them tighter; the man obviously had guessed she would do what she could.

For an instant her hands lingered over his.

"Step away now," the voice ordered.

Ana hesitated. And in that moment she leaned forward and kissed Ryder gently on his bruised cheek. There was a world of promise in that tiny kiss, and Ryder felt his pulse surge. He would get them out of this, somehow. For the first time in his life he had something he would die for.

But he was going to do his damnedest to live.

Chapter 21

"A loving little display. How touching," the voice said, the scorn practically bouncing off the walls.

Clearly he had no trouble seeing what was happening in the darkened room, Ryder thought. He suspected they used night goggles.

"Touching, but pointless," the voice said. "Leon!"

The man, who was apparently more than just a driver, stepped forward, crossing the room toward the voice. Moments later the lights in the room came on. Ryder had barely a moment to register the bare stone walls and floor of a small room in a very old building, because across the room stood the driver and in his hands was a duffel bag. A familiar duffel bag. A corner of a pink flowered blanket protruded from the unzipped opening.

"Maria," Ana cried.

"Don't move!" the voice shouted.

A heartfelt wail issued from the duffel, and Ryder's gut

knotted. She was so tiny, so helpless. His only consolation was that she didn't know enough to be afraid. But he knew she was in danger. His mind rapidly turned over possibilities as his hands worked at the rope binding his wrists, trying to get the proper alignment.

"How much do you want her back, Ana? What will you do to get her? How far will you go?" The disembodied voice taunted her.

"I will do anything to get my baby back," Ana said frantically.

"Ah, that is what I wanted to hear," the voice said. "Leon?"

The man holding the duffel stepped forward. Ana eagerly reached for it, but the man pulled it away. He set the bag down on the floor, then took a lethal-looking pistol from a side pocket. Ryder winced at the unseemly juxtaposition of the weapon and the innocent child.

Leon held the gun out to Ana. She stared at it, then at the man who held it, clearly startled.

"Take it," the voice ordered. "Show me how much you want your baby back. Will you truly sacrifice your noble lover?"

Ana gasped as Ryder's stomach clenched. Maybe he wasn't going to get out of this alive after all.

And without ever knowing what it would be like to be Ana's lover.

Oddly, that hurt more than the thought of impending death.

"Take it, sweet Ana. Take it, or I will have Leon use it on the brat."

With another gasp she grabbed the weapon, her gaze fastened on the splash of pink blanket.

"That's better. Now all you have to do is use it. Shoot him."

"You cannot mean that."

"Don't tell me what I can mean," the voice snapped,

sounding provoked. Interesting, Ryder thought. He'd been so blasé until now. Ana went very still, and he wondered if she'd noticed the change, too.

"You expect me to murder in cold blood?"

"I expect you to do what a good little mother would do. Save your child. Another man will come along for you to entice, seduce. You won't miss this one for long."

Ryder was watching Ana's face, trying to guess what she might do. At the same time he was working on the rope, hoping the melodrama playing out would give him cover. But for a moment he stopped sawing at his bonds, when he saw a familiar expression cross Ana's face. The expression he'd learned meant she was thinking, and quickly.

"Why are you doing this?" she asked.

"Do not question me!"

Again the snap, Ryder thought. He went back to working to free himself.

"Why do you wish him dead?"

Ryder wasn't sure what she was doing, asking all these questions, but since it was keeping Leon's eyes off him, he wasn't going to complain.

"He got in my way. Now do it, or you'll never see your baby alive."

"What will you do with her if I do not?"

The voice laughed. "Since she is female, I will train her to do what they are best suited for. And when she is old enough—perhaps thirteen or so—I will sell her to the highest bidder."

Fury spiked through Ryder. He fought it down, sensing that was exactly what the man wanted, that he wanted them provoked and angry…and helpless to do anything. He was feeding on that helplessness as a vampire would feed on the blood of his victims.

"Stop playing with us," Ana exclaimed. "You are like a cat with a mouse."

"Ah, but that is the fun of it, isn't it, *gatita?*"

Something flashed in Ana's eyes as the voice called her kitten. Some combination of knowledge, understanding, and anger that took Ryder's breath away. She looked as if the puzzle had suddenly fallen together in front of her eyes.

She knows, Ryder thought suddenly. She knows who this is.

And that quickly the entire landscape of the situation, and what had happened, shifted. Because there was only one explanation he could think of for her knowledge.

Ana's past had caught up with her.

"Shoot him now, or Leon will take that bag and throw it in the canal."

Ana's hands shook, but she lifted the gun. As if it had just occurred to her, she checked to see if it was truly loaded. Her face went pale, and Ryder guessed that meant it was.

She steadied the weapon with both hands. And slowly, she aimed it at Ryder.

He sucked in a breath, his gaze meeting hers over the sights of the weapon. Tears were brimming in her eyes, and he had the crazy thought that he had to make this easier for her. He couldn't bear the anguish in those beautiful dark eyes another moment.

"It's all right, Ana. I understand," he said.

And waited for her to do what she had to.

Anger, Ana thought, was a very useful emotion. Rage was dangerous, because it made you stop thinking. And she needed to think.

Gatita.

Kitten. Only one person in the world had ever called her that. A sweet, gentle nickname that had, in his hands, become an insult, a taunt, and finally a threat. And it had done so before today, in fact, from the moment she dared to question him, to ask for the truth about his activities, and his connection to her father.

Because she had no doubts; she knew with absolute certainty that her worst fears had materialized. That muffled voice belonged to Alberto Cardenas.

Her former fiancé.

Maria's father.

It was all clear now. Maria's kidnapping had not been a random happening, a crime of opportunity. It had been carefully planned and executed. Not because he wanted his daughter back—he had as little use for women as her father—but because she was his property. And no one stole from Alberto Cardenas.

She should have known better. Alberto would never accept that his woman had escaped from his grasp. It would be too big a blow to his manhood, and he would take it very personally. He had probably been looking for her, no doubt with her father's help, from the moment he'd discovered her gone.

And obviously their criminal network was very good at following orders. She had been a fool to think she could evade them.

But now there was more than her own life at stake. There was her child, the child she had promised to keep safe, to give a good life.

And Ryder.

God, Ryder. He had risked his life for her, and for Maria. And he had come here ready to make the sacrifice, to trade himself for her daughter. Even knowing what would likely happen, that it would probably mean his own death.

And in the moment when he had to believe she would kill him, he had thought only to ease her pain. To tell her he understood.

Determination flooded her. She might have been naïve once, but no more. And she knew she had one thing no one else had. Knowledge. Alberto didn't know for sure she'd guessed who he was. He might wonder if he had betrayed too much, but he thought her a fool and probably too stupid to pick up on it. But even if he did know she had guessed, it did not matter, because that was not the knowledge that mattered.

What mattered was that she knew Alberto, and knew exactly how to provoke him. She knew, as they said in America, how to push his buttons.

And push she would.

She could coax, she thought. Cajole, let him think she was cowed, and would show the proper respect now. He would enjoy making her crawl, she was certain. But would he believe her? She wasn't sure. And it would take too long. He would toy with her endlessly, and every moment with Maria so close and yet out of her reach was sheer agony.

Alberto's hair-trigger temper, on the other hand, was easy to provoke. And since he was obviously already furious with her, she had no doubt that even if she did coax him, the end result would be the same. He would kill Ryder—or make her do it. Then he would kill her, no doubt after reasserting his ownership in the worst possible, most painful and degrading way.

And Maria would be helplessly caught, destined for that horrific future her own father had planned for her.

Ana would not allow it. Alberto clearly thought her so useless, helpless, that he could put a loaded gun in her hands and make her follow his orders simply out of fear. So she would use his bad judgment against him.

"You are right," she said, as if after long consideration. "You are not a cat. Cats are at least brave enough to do their own hunting, kill their own prey."

The voice did not answer, but she heard a hiss as if he had sucked in a breath, coming over the speaker.

"You are a filthy vulture," she said, "a carrion eater, letting someone else do your dirty work."

"Quiet!"

Ana ignored the angry command. Ryder's eyes met hers again, and she saw understanding there once more; he realized what she was doing. She saw him glance around the room, as if noting the position of the two men who had brought them here. One was in front of them next to that priceless duffel bag on the floor and the other behind them, between them and the door through which they had entered. Then he looked at the only other door, the one at the far end of the room, over which the speaker the voice issued from had been placed.

"You hide behind this—" she gestured at the room "—afraid to even set foot in here, for fear a bound man and a useless woman will be too much for you to handle."

The voice swore at her in Spanish, a string of epithets she remembered well.

She heard Ryder whisper, too low for even Leon to hear. "I'm almost loose. Don't second-guess. Just shoot."

Ana's pulse leapt as adrenaline shot through her. She didn't know how he had done it, but it was both of them now, and the odds weren't quite so staggering.

"Coward." She spat out the word, letting every bit of her

contempt show. "Do you think your peons will not spread the word that you were too afraid to face a *woman?*"

Leon shifted uncomfortably, whether at being called a peon, or at the escalating tension Ana neither knew nor cared. She cared only about the black bag at his feet.

"Is that why you left Mexico? They found out your woman had gotten away from you, that you weren't man enough to keep her?"

"You are dead, *puta,* and I will do it with my own hands at your throat!"

She could almost hear the spittle as he shouted the word. Being called a whore again meant nothing to her; what mattered was that she heard the sound of footsteps over the speaker.

When the door beneath the speaker slammed open, things happened fast.

The man in front of them turned, startled to see his boss. Ryder, his hands somehow free, leapt at him, taking him down to the floor and rolling. Rolling him away from Maria, Ana realized as Alberto shouted.

"Shoot him!" he ordered the second man as he rushed toward Ana, his hands outstretched, fingers already curling as if they were around her throat. She wondered that she had ever thought him handsome; he was ugly, his face contorted by the evil at his core.

The second man hesitated, unable to get a clear shot. Ryder slammed the man who had given her the gun against the stone floor, knocking him out, then, in the same swift move, rolled once more and took the second armed man's feet out from under him.

Ana saw it only out of the corner of her eye; she was focused on the man coming at her across the room.

And on what she had to do.

Memories of all he'd done before, of what he'd done now flooded her, steeling her resolve and steadying her hand. She looked into the face of evil, and for a second, hesitated.

Don't second-guess. Just shoot.

She shot.

Chapter 22

Ana cuddled Maria to her breast, the hungry baby suckling with a fierce need that made her weep. She herself leaned against Ryder, sitting on the floor behind her, both she and her baby in the shelter of his arms.

"You're sure she's all right?" Ryder asked, sounding worried.

Ana had quickly checked the baby; she did not appear to have any injuries, but Ana would feel better when a doctor saw her and confirmed this.

"I think so." She smiled as the tiny fists kneaded her breast. She looked up at Ryder. He was watching her with such a rapt, gentle expression that she felt no embarrassment.

"I used to watch you, from a distance, when you would get up in the night to feed her. It was…beautiful."

Odd how the thought did not bother her, she thought. But there was a big difference between watching someone like a spy, and watching over her. She felt nothing but gladness that he had been there for them.

Again.

"I never intended to shoot you," Ana said, feeling suddenly anxious to be sure he knew that.

"If you'd had to, it would have been—" he began, but she hushed him.

"I would not. I knew you would do something, that you would not abandon Maria to such a fate."

He smiled then. "Good thing I learned about razor-edged belt buckles in prison. And that the room was dark enough I could slide the buckle to the back to get at the rope without being spotted."

"How strange, that if you had not been in prison to learn that, we would all be dead now."

He looked bemused all over again, then simply shook his head as if at the serendipity of life.

She frowned when the cell phone rang, destroying the moment. But she knew it was crucial that Ryder talk to the contact he had paged a few minutes before. When he answered, she heard him tell the man what had happened. She held her breath when he described the encounter that had resulted in the shooting; he had wanted to tell them he'd killed Alberto, but Ana refused to allow it, pointing out that a mother acting in defense of her baby was much less likely to be charged with a crime. His contact apparently agreed, as Ryder repeated for her benefit the man's assurances that no charges would be filed.

Ryder explained then what they had found here, not only the workings of the operation Alberto had begun here in Italy, but records outlining the entirety of the operation he had left behind on the Texas border, including names, dates—and most important the location of many of the kidnapped babies.

Ana heard him make arrangements to hand over everything to a local operative. Then he was silent, listening intently. His faced changed, and at last he said a quiet, "Thank you. I will."

He snapped the phone shut, and for a moment just sat there, looking at it.

"What did he say?"

"They're ecstatic," Ryder said with a crooked grin that took her breath away; she'd never seen him look like this, so carefree. "And I'm free."

Ana's eyes widened. "It is done? He said so?"

"He said 'You've got a second chance. Make it good.'" He reached out to stroke her hair. Then, gently, he brushed the back of his fingers over Maria's cheek. "I intend to do just that."

Ana's throat tightened. Soon, they would be busy, she guessed. Talking, explaining, showing what they'd found here. It would take time, no doubt. But she had that now.

And she had Ryder.

Ana sighed, and snuggled up to his warmth.

"I don't understand what happened the night she was born," Ryder said, sounding bemused. "But I feel like..."

"As if she is yours?"

He nodded, looking as if he were about to blush, Ana thought. She found it impossibly endearing.

Just as she found endearing that he'd wanted to take her for that symbol of romance in Venice, a gondola ride. She had to admit there was something quite romantic about it.

But nothing nearly as romantic as Ryder's assumption that of course Maria would come with them, because there was no way he was letting the baby out of his sight again for the foreseeable future.

"I have thought of her that way," she admitted. "As if there would forever be a connection between you and her."

There was a long, silent moment before Ryder said quietly, "And you, Ana?"

She hesitated for a moment, but only to search for the right words. There was no doubt in her mind that she had finally found what she thought would always elude her, a man she could love and trust completely. A man who would always be there for her and for Maria.

And no woman in the world could have had better proof of that than she had received today.

"I can only hope for that for myself," she said at last. "It is up to you."

He kissed her then, and it was everything she had known it would be; passionate, yes, and hot and arousing, but also achingly sweet, and full of a promise that was unlike any she had ever known, because this one she knew she could believe in.

When at last he broke the kiss and drew back, she could barely breathe.

"Do you want me, Ana?"

"So much," she answered, meaning it with all her heart and body, looking up into the dark, piercing eyes that had been the thing she remembered most about him from the night Maria was born.

He tightened his arms around her then, and she felt a tremor go through him. It thrilled her in a new sort of way, and she realized that this was only the beginning.

"When the doctor says it's all right…it will be good, Ana. I promise."

"I already know this," she said, feeling lighthearted enough to tease him a little.

As the oddly shaped boat moved along the canal, the

gondolier maintaining a discreet silence and distance, Ryder held her quietly for a long time.

"Do you believe in miracles, Ana?" he finally asked.

"I believe in you," she said.

"I've never been worth that," he said. "But now…"

"You have changed."

"I have." He shook his head. "I have my life back. And you and Maria to share it with. How lucky can one guy get?"

"You will be luckier yet," Ana promised.

"Can't be," Ryder said with a chuckle.

"Yes," Ana insisted. "Because soon you will have your brother and sister back."

Ryder went still.

"They will know what you have done, and they will see the man you have become. And they will accept you for who you are now, and forgive whatever you might have been in the past. You will have the homecoming you deserve. This is my promise to you, Ryder Grady Colton."

For a long, silent moment he just looked at her. She held his gaze, letting every bit of what she was feeling show.

He threw back his head and laughed, a loud, joyous laugh unlike anything she'd ever heard from him. It lifted her heart and her hopes, told her she was right, that together they could conquer anything.

"If anyone can do that, you can," he said.

"I will," she said determinedly.

"Damn. Boots is going to give me that smug, I-told-you-so look again," Ryder said.

She wasn't sure what that meant, but she was too content at the moment to ask. Later. Nothing mattered just now except that the three of them were here, together, and safe.

It didn't matter, Ana thought as the sunset turned the

water to fire and they floated under the famous Bridge of Sighs, that they were at the moment living a romantic cliché.

Clichés, she thought, became clichés because they were the best way to express something.

And the best way she could think of to express what she was feeling right now, was to kiss the man she loved.

So she did.

"...Colton campaign's swing through Texas is being anticipated with great excitement, now that disgraced Governor Daniels is out of the election picture."

The man watching the television report grinned. A dark, roiling sort of joy filled him. He nearly laughed aloud with glee as he watched the video clip of the candidate moving through the crowd, shaking hands, smiling, eating up the adulation like the pig he was.

It was all coming together. The two people at the top of his list, the two people he most wanted within his grasp, were both going to be within reach at the same time. Obviously he was on the right track, this was meant to be.

This was the time, and the place. All his work, all his planning, was finally going to bring him his soul's deepest desire.

He would finally have his payback.

* * * * *

Don't miss the exciting conclusion of
THE COLTONS: FAMILY FIRST *with next month's*
A HERO OF HER OWN by Carla Cassidy!

Celebrate 60 years of pure reading pleasure with Harlequin® Books!

Harlequin Romance® is celebrating by showering you with DIAMOND BRIDES *in February 2009. Six stories that promise to bring a touch of sparkle to your life, with diamond proposals and dazzling weddings, sparkling brides and gorgeous grooms!*

Enjoy a sneak peek at Caroline Anderson's TWO LITTLE MIRACLES, available February 2009 from Harlequin Romance®.

"I'VE FOUND HER."

Max froze.

It was what he'd been waiting for since June, but now—now he was almost afraid to voice the question. His heart stalling, he leaned slowly back in his chair and scoured the investigator's face for clues. "Where?" he asked, and his voice sounded rough and unused, like a rusty hinge.

"In Suffolk. She's living in a cottage."

Living. His heart crashed back to life, and he sucked in a long, slow breath. All these months he'd feared—

"Is she well?"

"Yes, she's well."

He had to force himself to ask the next question. "Alone?"

The man paused. "No. The cottage belongs to a man called John Blake. He's working away at the moment, but he comes and goes."

God. He felt sick. So sick he hardly registered the next few words, but then gradually they sank in. "She's got *what?"*

"Babies. Twin girls. They're eight months old."

"Eight—?" he echoed under his breath. "They must be his."

He was thinking out loud, but the P.I. heard and corrected him.

"Apparently not. I gather they're hers. She's been there since mid-January last year, and they were born during the summer—June, the woman in the post office thought. She was more than helpful. I think there's been a certain amount of speculation about their relationship."

He'd just bet there had. God, he was going to kill her. Or Blake. Maybe both of them.

"Of course, looking at the dates, she was presumably pregnant when she left you, so they could be yours, or she could have been having an affair with this Blake character before..."

He glared at the unfortunate P.I. "Just stick to your job. I can do the math," he snapped, swallowing the unpalatable possibility that she'd been unfaithful to him before she'd left. "Where is she? I want the address."

"It's all in here," the man said, sliding a large envelope across the desk to him. "With my invoice."

"I'll get it seen to. Thank you."

"If there's anything else you need, Mr. Gallagher, any further information—"

"I'll be in touch."

"The woman in the post office told me Blake was away at the moment, if that helps," he added quietly, and opened the door.

Max stared down at the envelope, hardly daring to open

it, but when the door clicked softly shut behind the P.I., he eased up the flap, tipped it and felt his breath jam in his throat as the photos spilled out over the desk.

Oh, lord, she looked gorgeous. Different, though. It took him a moment to recognize her, because she'd grown her hair, and it was tied back in a ponytail, making her look younger and somehow freer. The blond highlights were gone, and it was back to its natural soft golden-brown, with a little curl in the end of the ponytail that he wanted to thread his finger through and tug, just gently, to draw her back to him.

Crazy. She'd put on a little weight, but it suited her. She looked well and happy and beautiful, but oddly, considering how desperate he'd been for news of her for the past year—one year, three weeks and two days, to be exact—it wasn't only Julia who held his attention after the initial shock. It was the babies sitting side by side in a supermarket trolley. Two identical and absolutely beautiful little girls.

* * * * *

COMING NEXT MONTH

#1547 SCANDAL IN COPPER LAKE—Marilyn Pappano
When Anamaria Duquesne returns to Copper Lake to discover the truth about her mother's death and her still-missing baby sister, she doesn't count on running into Robbie Calloway. Suspecting her of being a con artist, Robbie agrees to keep an eye on Anamaria, but he can't help entertaining feelings for her. And a relationship with Anamaria would be anything but easy....

#1548 A HERO OF HER OWN—Carla Cassidy
The Coltons: Family First
From the moment she arrives in town, Jewel Mayfair catches the attention of veterinarian Quinn Logan. They're both overcoming tragic pasts, but as Jewel lets down her guard to give in to passion with Quinn, mysterious events make her question her choices. Should she take a second chance on love, or is Quinn the last man she should trust?

#1549 THE REDEMPTION OF RAFE DIAZ—Maggie Price
Dates with Destiny
Businesswoman Allie Fielding never thought she'd see Rafe Diaz again—at least not on the outside of a prison cell! But when Allie stumbles over the body of a murdered customer, the now-exonerated P.I. she helped put behind bars shows up to question her. His investigation stirs up a past Rafe thought was behind him—and unlocks a passion that could put them both at risk.

#1550 HEART AT RISK—Ana Leigh
Bishop's Heroes
A family was the furthest thing from Kurt Bolen's mind, yet when he discovers he has a son, he'll do whatever it takes to make the boy and his mother his own. But someone is after Kurt, and in the midst of rekindling their romance, he and Maddie must band together to protect their son and fight for their future.

SRSCNMBPA0109